D1403062

# WELCOM

## AMAZING ACADEMY.
### SURVIVAL
### SCHOOL OF
### EXPLORATION AND SURVIVAL

As you would expect from the school that teaches you what you really need to know, this course on exploration and survival gives you all you need to start exploring and . . . er . . . surviving. Along with this manual, your Amazing Academy kit should contain the following items:

**HANDS-ON BOOK • ID CARD • CAMPUS MAP • DOG TAG**

**PLEASE CHECK THAT ALL THESE ITEMS ARE PRESENT AND CORRECT BEFORE PROCEEDING. YOUR SURVIVAL MAY DEPEND ON IT!**

READY TO GO?
GOOD – START EXPLORING!

**IMPORTANT NOTES FOR ALL STUDENTS**
WE MUST WARN YOU THAT MANY OF THE EXERCISES IN THIS BOOK SHOULD BE UNDERTAKEN WITH EXTREME CARE. WE'RE AWARE THAT NOT ALL OF OUR STUDENTS ARE FORTUNATE ENOUGH TO HAVE THE AMAZING ACADEMY TUTORS ON HAND TO ADVISE THEM. SO IF YOU ARE GOING TO TRY OUT SOME OF THE TIPS AND EXERCISES IN THIS COURSE, WE RECOMMEND THAT YOU APPOINT A PARENT AS A HOME TUTOR TO HELP YOU WITH THE TASKS. THEY MIGHT LEARN SOMETHING AS WELL. WHEN YOU SEE THE HOME TUTOR SYMBOL IT'S TIME TO GET THEIR HELP.

**THE COURSE**

# HOW IT WORKS

The course is broken into four sections. Each section has a number of lessons, often with an exercise or test for you to do. Successful completion of the test will earn you credits that will go towards your final score. (You can keep a record of your credits in the Hands-on book accompanying this manual.) All tasks are self-assessed, which means you grade yourself. Our staff are way too busy and important to be doing that sort of thing, thank you very much. (And no cheating, either.)

## SECTION 1: SURVIVAL BASICS
**Tutor in Survival: Ray "Wildman" Dixon**

This section covers the essentials of survival: food, fire, shelter, and water. You'll learn how to build shelters, hunt for food, and avoid dying from hunger or thirst.

## SECTION 2: NAVIGATION AND MAPMAKING
**Tutor in Intentional and Accidental Navigation: Bjorn Sigurdsson**

This section takes you through all kinds of navigational techniques. You'll learn how to use a compass, how to read and make maps, and how to avoid getting lost while going shopping.

## SECTION 3: EXPLORATION – HISTORY AND PRACTICE
**Tutor in Exploration History: Paolo Marco**

This section introduces you to exploration, past and present. Learn about the great explorers of the past, find out about trade and language, and plan your own expedition!

## SECTION 4: GADGETS AND EQUIPMENT
**Tutor in Gadgets and Equipment: Lt. Col. Billy MacMasters**

This section teaches you what equipment you need and how to use it. You'll learn how to use and take care of everything from satellite phones to snowshoes, from hammocks to huskies.

# MEET THE TUTORS

## DIRECTOR OF STUDIES

# Ernst Von Strudelhopf

**"Von Strudelhopf of the Antarctic,"** as he was known, was the first explorer to reach the South Pole by the notorious "reverse" route (that is, going via Toronto, where he had to do some shopping.) A master of survival in the howling wastelands of places such as Alaska, the Arctic Tundra, and Cleveland, he once escaped being eaten by polar bears by disguising himself as a penguin. Although it meant sitting on a nest for three months, it was, he says, "better than being eaten."

- Age: Not telling
- Height: 6 ft 5 in (1.96 meters)
- Skills: Arctic survival, marine navigation, soccer tricks, pasta-making

Von Strudelhopf, disguised as a penguin, Princess Elizabeth Lands, 1973

# VON STRUDELHOPF ESCAPES DEATH. AGAIN.

### Tjikkennibblets, Finland, May 22 1961

The famous explorer Ernst Von Strudelhopf is today recovering after his latest expedition – to climb Mount Kilimanjaro – ended in failure. "The main difficulty," he told reporters, "was the fact that Mount Kilimanjaro is in Africa, and I was in Lapland. This only goes to show how important planning is. Not to mention holding the map the right way up." After his dramatic escape, during which he survived by eating moss and seagull eggs, the intrepid explorer has vowed to help others who might be in a similar plight. "I want to start a school for explorers," he told us, "so I can share the things I've learned. Things like "don't go to Lapland when you're supposed to be in Tanzania.'"

## TUTOR IN SURVIVAL

# Ray "Wildman" Dixon

**Ray "Wildman" Dixon** has spent many years living on his own in the wild. (Unlike his brothers Ben "Not-very-wildman" Dixon, and Sam "Staying-in-a-Motorhome" Dixon.) He will teach you how to make shelters, what foods you can eat to survive, and how to treat wounds without having to amputate your own leg. He once survived three weeks on a glacier by just drinking boiled ice and eating moss. His publications include *101 Ways to Cook Moss* and *The Low-Fat Moss Diet*.

- Age: 45 years
- Height: 6 ft 3 in (1.91 meters)
- Weight: 196 lb (14 stone)
- Skills: survival, hunting, crochet

## TUTOR IN INTENTIONAL AND ACCIDENTAL NAVIGATION

# Bjorn Sigurdsson

**Bjorn Sigurdsson's** ancestors were famous Norse explorers. Many discovered new lands—sometimes when they actually meant to, but more often when they were completely lost or suffering from the aftereffects of too many sweets. Many were also violent, marauding brutes, but as Bjorn says, "We've all calmed down since then." (Although students are advised not to let him near an axe.) Bjorn will teach you techniques for finding out where you are, where you're going and, importantly, where the nearest reindeer-meat restaurant is.

- Age: Unknown
- Height: 5 ft 7 in (1.7 meters)
- Weight: 168 lb (12 stone)
- Skills: navigation, astronomy, expert sailor

## TUTOR IN EXPLORATION HISTORY

# Paolo Marco

**Paolo Marco** is an expert on exploration past and present. He can teach you how to learn the language of the country you're in, and, more importantly, how to make money from this. His ancestors were pioneers in global trade, traveling thousands of miles to buy silk from China, spices from India, and donuts from the supermarket. Paolo is well-versed in exploration history, having heard many tales from his grandfather. "Sometimes," he says, "I even stayed awake."

- Age: 61 years
- Height: 4 ft 10 in (1.47 meters)
- Weight: 280 lb (20 stone)
- Skills: linguistics, trading, pasta-making

## TUTOR IN GADGETS AND EQUIPMENT

# Lt. Col. Billy MacMasters

**Billy MacMasters** is the youngest officer in the army (age 11). Lt. Col. MacMasters is a former Quartermaster and Storemaster for SAS, the US Marines and the crack commando unit of the Boy Scouts. Despite his age, he knows all about equipping expeditions to the toughest places. His illustrated lecture, "101 Uses of a Fork," is always a highlight for the academic year.

- Age: 11 yrs
- Height: 4 ft 8 in (1.42 meters)
- Weight: 98 lb (7 stone)
- Skills: electrical engineering, satellite recalibration, and tree-climbing

# FINDING YOUR WAY AROUND

Welcome to the school—and your first task is to explore the campus! This map will show you where everything is and also help you avoid getting lost which, let's face it, is always a bit embarrassing for would-be explorers.

Observation deck

Giant telescope

## LIBRARY AND MAP ROOM

Open 9:00 a.m.–9:00 p.m. Closed Thursdays and the Librarian's birthday. Here in the Map Room we have maps of all the known regions and countries of the world, and quite a few made-up places as well. We also have atlases of all shapes and sizes and several large globes.

Director's office (only reached by ladder)

Desert survival training. Do not attempt to leave building without water, sunblock, and a camel.

Instrument room

Lost property

## OASIS, AMAZING ACADEMY DESERT SURVIVAL AREA

Animal outfitting desk

West of the Explorer's School main complex. The oasis is just one of the many challenging regions in the Amazing Academy campus that we will be using for survival training. We also be using other extremely hazardous areas such as the Amazing Academy jungle, the mountains, and the caretaker's office.

Main entrance, reception, and offices

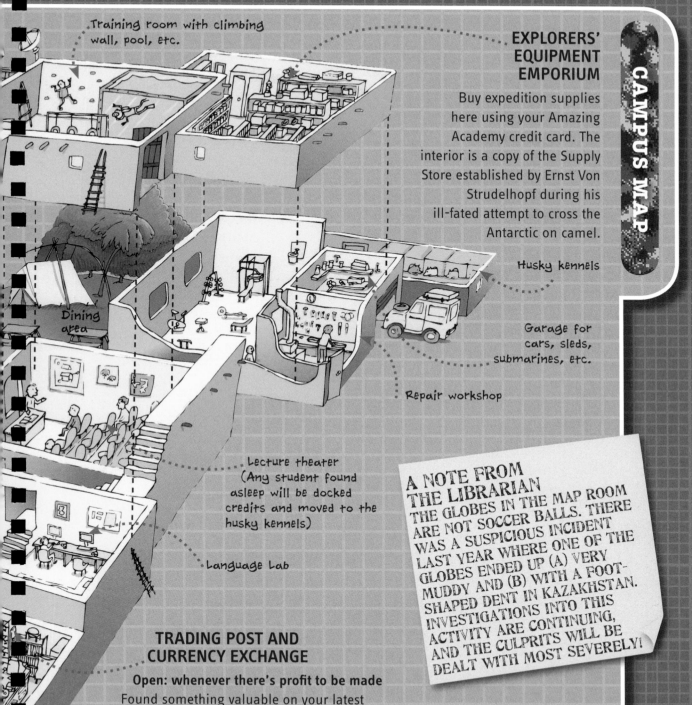

Training room with climbing wall, pool, etc.

Dining area

## EXPLORERS' EQUIPMENT EMPORIUM

Buy expedition supplies here using your Amazing Academy credit card. The interior is a copy of the Supply Store established by Ernst Von Strudelhopf during his ill-fated attempt to cross the Antarctic on camel.

Husky kennels

Garage for cars, sleds, submarines, etc.

Repair workshop

Lecture theater (Any student found asleep will be docked credits and moved to the husky kennels)

Language Lab

## A NOTE FROM THE LIBRARIAN

THE GLOBES IN THE MAP ROOM ARE NOT SOCCER BALLS. THERE WAS A SUSPICIOUS INCIDENT LAST YEAR WHERE ONE OF THE GLOBES ENDED UP (A) VERY MUDDY AND (B) WITH A FOOT-SHAPED DENT IN KAZAKHSTAN. INVESTIGATIONS INTO THIS ACTIVITY ARE CONTINUING, AND THE CULPRITS WILL BE DEALT WITH MOST SEVERELY!

## TRADING POST AND CURRENCY EXCHANGE

**Open: whenever there's profit to be made**
Found something valuable on your latest expedition? Furs? Gold? A two-headed monkey? This is the place to trade it in. Items can be traded for supplies, or for rare goods found by other students. Any pupil found trading counterfeit goods will be severely reprimanded. (Unless they're very good at it, in which case they will be transferred to the School of Spying, where they admire that sort of thing.)

EQUIPMENT

# EQUIPMENT CHECKLIST

Preparation is the most vital phase of any expedition. Survival is a matter of being prepared. All explorers need to plan as much as possible for the situations they will be facing and the type of equipment they will need. You will find much more on equipment in the Gadgets and Equipment section. But to get you started, here is a checklist of basic equipment that no student explorer should be without.

- ☐ Cell phone or satellite phone
- ☐ Solar panel for recharging batteries
- ☐ Basic survival kit (see p.10)
- ☑ Compass
- ☑ First-aid kit
- ☑ Knife (see p.52)
- ☑ Notebook and pen
- ☑ Atlas

This will get you started. Feel free to put your own kit together, or choose one of the completed kits from the Trading Post.

VON STRUDELHOPF SAYS, "A GOOD ATLAS IS A FANTASTIC START FOR ANY STUDENT EXPLORER. THIS WILL BE USED IN YOUR NAVIGATION CLASSES AND WILL HELP YOU TO PLAN WHERE YOU WANT TO GO AND HOW TO GET THERE. PERSONALLY, I HAVE ALWAYS FAVORED KIPPERBUNG'S REALLY ACCURATE WORLD ATLAS. I KNOW IT'S NOT VERY ACCURATE, BUT I LIKE THE COLORS. THERE ARE MANY ATLASES IN THE MAP ROOM, OF COURSE. AND GLOBES, WHICH ARE NOT TO BE USED AS SOCCER BALLS, REMEMBER."

# SURVIVAL BASICS

You're alone. In the wilderness. No shelter, no food, and no one to help you. Not even your favorite teddy bear. (Mine is called Mr. Snookums.) Nothing to help you survive except your own skill. What would you do? How would you survive? In this section I'm going to teach you what you need to know. It won't make survival certain, but you will at least stand a chance. We're going to look at the four basic needs for survival: food, fire, shelter, and water. We're going to get together a basic and a more advanced survival kit. We're going to look at how to stay healthy. We're going to stay strong, stay focused. We're going to make it through this thing together. Why? Because Mr. Snookums needs us. We're doing it for him.

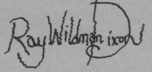

Ray "Wildman" Dixon

Mr. Snookums

## IN THIS SECTION

1. CREATE A BASIC SURVIVAL KIT
2. HOW TO BUILD A SHELTER
3. HOW TO MAKE A FIRE
4. HOW TO AVOID DYING OF THIRST
5. HOW TO AVOID DYING OF HUNGER
6. HOW TO COOK FOOD WITHOUT A KITCHEN
7. HOW TO MAKE AN EFFICIENT CAMP

**SURVIVAL KIT**

# CREATE A BASIC SURVIVAL KIT

**The first thing we need to do is be prepared. If you're prepared for the worst, then when the worst happens, you'll . . . er . . . be prepared for it. So lesson one is building a basic survival kit. All the items below can fit into a small container, such as a small, waterproof plastic box.**

## WATERPROOF MATCHES

Specialized waterproof matches are good, but expensive. You can make your own by dipping the head of ordinary matches in parrafin, clear nail polish, or shellac.

## CANDLE

Don't be stuck without light. Also good for starting a fire, as it doesn't go out as quickly as matches.

## MAGNIFYING GLASS

Useful for starting a fire from direct sunlight. And for identifying just precisely what that horrible green thing is crawling up your leg.

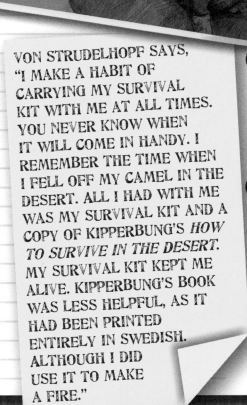

## NEEDLES AND THREAD

Learn how to repair your clothes. A stitch in time could save your life.

## COMPASS

One of the most important items in your kit. A glow-in-the-dark dial compass is best.

## FIRST-AID KIT

General items include bandages, gauze, tape, thread, string, first-aid spray, insect repellant, and sunscreen.

## ENERGY SUPPLY

A bag of jelly beans gives an instant energy rush from the sugar.

## KNIFE

A good knife is a must for any explorer, but you should always have parental approval before carrying one.

VON STRUDELHOPF SAYS, "I MAKE A HABIT OF CARRYING MY SURVIVAL KIT WITH ME AT ALL TIMES. YOU NEVER KNOW WHEN IT WILL COME IN HANDY. I REMEMBER THE TIME WHEN I FELL OFF MY CAMEL IN THE DESERT. ALL I HAD WITH ME WAS MY SURVIVAL KIT AND A COPY OF KIPPERBUNG'S *HOW TO SURVIVE IN THE DESERT*. MY SURVIVAL KIT KEPT ME ALIVE. KIPPERBUNG'S BOOK WAS LESS HELPFUL, AS IT HAD BEEN PRINTED ENTIRELY IN SWEDISH. ALTHOUGH I DID USE IT TO MAKE A FIRE."

# THE EXPANDED SURVIVAL KIT

**The Expanded Survival Kit fits easily into a large pouch or small backpack. In addition to the Basic Survival Kit, you will need:**

SURVIVAL KIT

### MESS PAN

A good mess pan or multipurpose pan will serve a wide variety of uses, from boiling water to cooking fish. Aluminium pans are the lightest.

### FUEL

Solid fuel can serve as fire starters or as replacement fuel when wood is not obtainable. A wide range of small, portable stoves are available.

### FLASHLIGHT

You don't need a huge, heavy flashlight; small flashlights can be very powerful. Keep the batteries in your flashlight. If you're extra cautious, reverse the last battery so that, if the flashlight is accidentally turned on, the batteries will not run out.

### FLUORESCENT MARKER

A piece of bright material which can be used to signal a long distance away.

### SURVIVAL BAG

A large bag which will keep you insulated and reduce heat loss. The best ones are made from reflective material, which reflects your body heat back at you. If you can't find that, an ordinary blanket will keep you warm.

### NOTEBOOK AND PEN

Keep a survival log. Write notes. Draw maps. Write down whatever you have eaten or drunk. That way if you do eat the wrong things and are found, medics will know how to treat you.

> THE REAL PROS ALSO ADD:
> ★ FISH HOOKS AND LINE – WHERE THERE'S WATER THERE'S FISH. (EXCEPT IN THE DEAD SEA.)
> ★ WATER-STERILIZING TABLETS – HANDY FOR SITUATIONS WHERE YOU CANNOT FIND A SUPPLY OF FRESH WATER.
> ★ SALT TABLETS – KEEPING UP YOUR SALT LEVEL IS VITAL.

## EXERCISES 1.1 & 1.2
### "WATERPROOF MATCHES" AND "CREATE A BASIC SURVIVAL KIT"
### HANDS-ON BOOK PP.2-3
### CREDITS: 15+2 FOR EXTRA ITEMS

# HOW TO BUILD A SHELTER

In any survival scenario, you will need a dry, secure shelter. Shelters need to be well insulated, protected from the elements (such as wind, rain, or snow), and have a space where you can make a fire. First, make sure the surrounding area has the basic material you need, especially a water supply, materials for a fire, and shelter from strong winds. Then build your shelter!

## SOME IDEAS FOR WILDERNESS SHELTERS

### Natural shelters

Get help from nature whenever you can. The first thing is to look for natural shelters such as caves or overhanging cliffs. If you find a cave, tie a piece of string to a rock at the entrance to be sure that you can find your way out. Move carefully! The cave might be occupied by dangerous beasts (bears, wolves, very savage bunnies, etc.) Build your fire near the cave's mouth to prevent animals from entering.

### Fallen tree shelter

Find a fallen tree—the larger the better. Then dig out the natural pit beneath it and line it with bark or branches from other trees. You can also make a basic lean-to against any large, solid object, e.g., rocks, an old wall, etc.

Lay strong branches to support the roof

Scoop a hollow on the leeward side (the side away from the wind)

### Rock house

If you have a good supply of rocks (e.g., from a rocky coastal area) you can make a rock wall in the shape of a U. Then cover the roof with driftwood and a tarp for protection. No tarp? Seaweed will also work well.

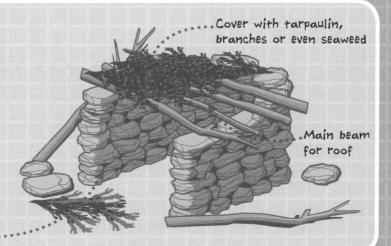

Cover with tarpaulin, branches or even seaweed

Main beam for roof

U-shaped wall, built out of stones (biggest stones on bottom)

## Sheet shelter

Of course, building a shelter is easier if you are prepared, which is why explorers should carry large, lightweight plastic sheets with them whenever possible.

Because then you can do this:
1. Tie a line between two trees.
2. Hang the plastic sheet over the line. Secure sheet with either stakes or heavy stones.
3. If the sheet is long enough, curl it under you to provide a dry surface for bedding. (You can use dry bracken or leaves as bedding—avoid lying on the cold ground.)

Mr. Snookums

Plastic sheeting over the top

Tree trunk

Sheeting curled under to provide sleeping area

Secure sheeting with stakes or rocks

VON STRUDELHOPF SAYS, "THE KEY THING FOR A SHELTER IS THAT IT IS WATERPROOF. ANIMAL HIDE IS EXCELLENT FOR THIS, BUT MY ADVICE IS TO REMOVE IT FROM THE ANIMAL FIRST. I ONCE SPENT THREE WEEKS LIVING INSIDE A DEAD YAK, AND IT WAS NOT PLEASANT."

YAK

1. Find Yak (they live in Tibet)
2. Find some sticks for support
3. peg yak to s...

take warm socks (in cold)
TIBET AIRLINES 0870 442002

LICHEN (chewisher!)
HERBS
COARSE GRASS

HOW TO TRAP YAK!
THE YAK FEEDS ON

## EXERCISE 1.3
### "BUILD A SHELTER"
### HANDS-ON BOOK P.4
### CREDITS: 20

# HOW TO MAKE A FIRE

Fire can mean the difference between life and death. Being able to make a fire means that you will be able to cook food, boil water, keep animals away, and stay warm. To make a fire you will need tinder, kindling and fuel.

## WARNING
STUDENTS ARE ADVISED THAT THEY WILL NEED THE HELP OF THEIR HOME TUTOR FOR ANYTHING TO DO WITH FIRE-LIGHTING ETC. FIRE CAN WARM YOU AND SAVE YOUR LIFE, BUT IT CAN ALSO KILL. DO NOT ATTEMPT TO LIGHT A FIRE WITHOUT YOUR HOME TUTOR PRESENT.

## PREPARING A FIREPLACE
1. Choose a site that is sheltered.
2. Clear the area. Important: clear twigs, leaves, and other debris in a circle at least 6 ft 6 in (2 meters) in diameter.
3. Make a hearth. If the ground is dry, you can use the earth; otherwise, make a hearth of rocks and stones. Do not use wet rocks, or any that crack when you bang them together—they may explode when heated.

## MAKING YOUR FIRE
Fire consists of three elements: tinder, kindling, and fuel.

- **Tinder** is any material that lights easily and quickly: dried grass, wood shavings, dried leaves, pulverized fir cones, newspaper, even old birds' nests. (Remove the bird first—they get very upset otherwise.)
- **Kindling** is material that catches fire easily, but burns longer than tinder. This will be small twigs, soft wood, etc.
- **Fuel** is what you're actually going to burn. Use the driest wood you can find to get the fire going. When it's established you can add damp or green wood. You can also burn coal, peat, even dried animal dung.

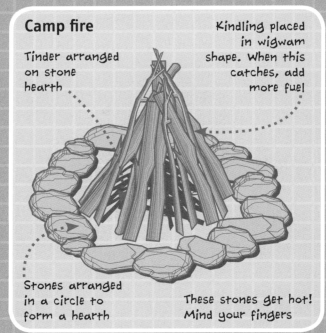

**Camp fire**

Tinder arranged on stone hearth

Kindling placed in wigwam shape. When this catches, add more fuel

Stones arranged in a circle to form a hearth

These stones get hot! Mind your fingers

## LIGHTING THE FIRE
Matches are the best way. There are other ways, such as using a flint, or rubbing two sticks together, but survival is hard enough without all that, thank you. If you're in a hot region use your magnifying glass to focus the sun on your kindling. Once it begins to smoke, blow on it gently. However, providing you have your survival kit with you, with your waterproof matches, you should be OK.

## Fire pit

When the wind is strong, you can make a trench or fire pit. Dig a trench in the ground, fill the base with rocks and arrange the fire on top of that.

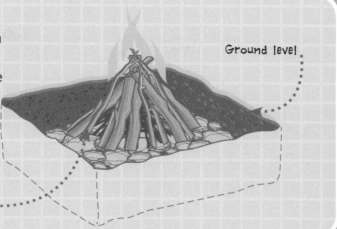

Ground level

Pit filled with layer of stones, then kindling wood

## OTHER WAYS OF KEEPING WARM

- Blankets are good.
- If you are in wet conditions, keep one set of clothes completely dry for sleeping in.
  Wear your wet clothes during the day.
- Warm food and drink will help you.

## WARNING

DO NOT LIGHT A FIRE IN VERY DRY CONDITIONS. YOU COULD EASILY START A FOREST FIRE THAT WILL GET OUT OF CONTROL. NEVER LEAVE YOUR FIRE UNATTENDED. IT COULD GO OUT. OR IT COULD SPREAD.

VON STRUDELHOPF SAYS, "BREWING A CUP OF TEA IS EXCELLENT FOR KEEPING WARM. IT WARMS YOU AND QUENCHES THIRST, AND IF YOU PILE IN THE SUGAR IT'S GOOD FOR SHOCK. ALSO IT SHOWS THAT, WHEREVER YOU FIND YOURSELF, YOU STILL HAVE STANDARDS."

## EXERCISE 1.4
### "DESIGN A FIRE"
### HANDS-ON BOOK P.5
### CREDITS: 5

# HOW TO AVOID DYING OF THIRST

So you've found shelter, and you've created fire. Mr. Snookums is safe and dry. The next thing is to find water, because water helps you to stay alive. Without food, you might be able to survive for three weeks, but without water, you won't last three days. So here's the most important part: don't wait till you've run out of water before you start to look for it. Make it a priority to find a water source and then work hard to make sure that the water is clean. The basic rule is that fast-flowing water is almost always better than still water, and water coming out of the ground is better than water running along the ground.

## FINDING WATER

Here are some places where you will find water:

- Water runs downhill, so go into valleys to look for streams and pools. (If you ever see water running uphill, you're probably upside down.) If there is no pool or river, try digging a hole—there may be water gathered under the surface.
- Be suspicious of any pool with no vegetation growing around it, or where there are animal bones. It may be polluted or poisonous.
- Rainwater is drinkable—you just need a method of collecting it. If you have made a shelter, put containers under the edge of the roof to catch water running off.
- Melting ice rather than snow gives you more water for less heat. If you have to melt snow, do it a little at a time.
- On coasts, dig above the sea line (i.e., where the high tide reaches to). Dig until you reach moist sand, then let the water gather. Freshwater floats on top of salty water. You might also find freshwater streams running into the sea, or water running down rock faces.
- In climates that are hot during the day and cold at night, the air condenses. Tie a cloth or hang clothing outside to act as a sponge, and then wring it out.

## FILTERING AND PURIFYING WATER

Water needs to be filtered and purified. Filtering means taking all the gunge out of the water—all the muck and twigs, etc. Purification means making it fit to drink. You can buy water filters and purification tablets that you can carry with you.

## WATER FROM TREES

Trees store huge amounts of water in their roots from deep underground. You can use evaporation to get some of that water for yourself. Here's how:

1. Choose a healthy looking branch with lots of leaves.
2. Tie a plastic bag around the branch, with a corner at the bottom to collect condensation.
3. Wait overnight. In the morning you should see some water in the bottom of the bag.

Tie bag securely round branch

Low corner of the bag collects water

## MAKING A WATER FILTER

You can make a simple water filter yourself. All you need is layers of material through which the water will pass and which can take out all the grungy bits.

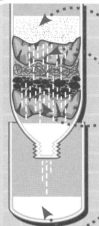

Dirty Water in here

Layer of cloth at top; something like a hankie, or a sock!

Layers of gravel, moss, charcoal, and sand, with another layer of cloth at the bottom

Clean Water in here

A water filter made out of a plastic bottle. The bottle is cut into two sections; and the top half is stuffed with layers of cloth, moss, gravel, and charcoal. The water is poured in the top and comes out clear.

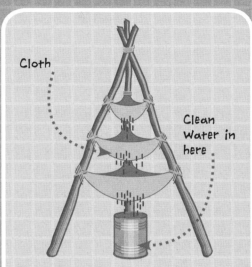

Cloth

Clean Water in here

A tripod system, in which cloth containing different filtering materials is tied across a tripod. The water drips down from level to level and into the can at the bottom.

## WATER PURIFICATION

Now you have to purify it.
1. Boil it. To be on the safe side boil it for 20 minutes or so.
2. After boiling, add water-purification tablets.
Boiled water can taste flat. This is because it has lost oxygen. However, you can add a bit more sparkle to it by simply pouring it from one container to another.

## EXERCISE 1.5
### "PLASTIC BOTTLE WATER FILTER"
### HANDS-ON BOOK P.6
### CREDITS: 10

# HOW TO AVOID DYING OF HUNGER

**You might be surprised to know that food is the least important element of survival situations, since human beings can survive for several weeks without it. However, without food you will become weak, more likely to get ill, and too dizzy to perform important tasks. So, at some point, you will need to eat.**

The best course of action is to carry survival rations with you. These are packets of food that only require water or keep for a long time. But what if you haven't got them with you? Well, there are other ways to find food.

You can:

- set traps to find meat
- find edible plants and fungi
- catch fish

You can even eat insects such as maggots – yum!

Yummy maggots. Very good fried. Can be roasted, but stuffing them is tricky.

Finding food in the wild depends on your surroundings. If you are stranded in the desert, it's harder to find food than in the forest. Here's an idea of what's available.

## PLANTS AND BERRIES

The important thing here is to know what you can eat and what you can't. This is an advanced skill that is not covered on this course. The basic rule is: never eat anything you cannot positively identify. Don't know what the berry is? Don't eat it. For finding this kind of food, the best thing is to buy a specialized book and practice your identification skills.

## HUNTING

Setting snares, traps, nets, and set lines will assist you in finding food to help with your survival. Trails are excellent places to set snares. Animal tracks offer information pertaining to the type of animal, its size, and the direction it was headed. Following these tracks will often lead to water holes and feeding grounds where you may use your traps or snares. Or you can lie in wait at water holes and use a homemade spear or throwing club.

RAY DIXON SAYS, "THERE ARE LOTS OF BOOKS OUT THERE TO HELP YOU IDENTIFY WHAT FOOD IS SAFE TO EAT. DO NOT, HOWEVER, BUY KIPPERBUNG'S FOOD FROM THE WILD. IT CONTAINS SEVERAL ERRORS. FOR EXAMPLE, A MUSHROOM THAT IT CLAIMS IS 'IDEAL FOR OMELETTES' WILL IN FACT TURN YOU BLUE AND MAKE ALL YOUR TOES FALL OFF."

## WARNING
IN MOST PLACES IT IS ILLEGAL TO SET FISH OR ANIMAL TRAPS. THESE ARE SURVIVAL SKILLS FOR EMERGENCY SITUATIONS. DO NOT TRY THEM AT ANY OTHER TIME, AND NEVER EAT ANYTHING YOU'RE NOT SURE IS SAFE.

## FISH

Survival fishing is different from normal fishing. Survival fishing is often done without you even being there. It's more like trapping or snaring.

If you have fishhooks and lines, you can bait lots of hooks, string them on a line across the river or stream, and leave them to work. (You can make fishhooks out of all kinds of things, including thorns, bits of old wire, bone, seashells, etc. )

If you are near shallow water (about waist deep) where the fish are large and plentiful, you can spear them.

## A FISH TRAP BUILT IN A RIVER

This trap relies on the fact that fish are too stupid to go back the way they came. The stones "shepherd" the fish into the holding area. From there they can be caught by hand or speared.

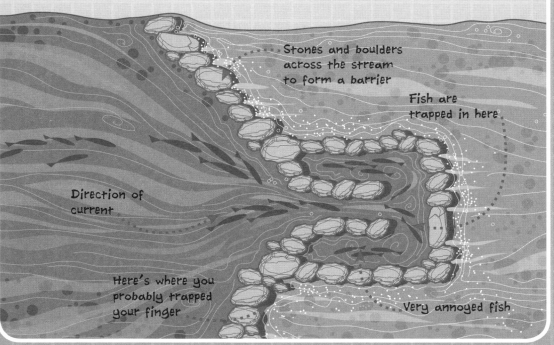

Stones and boulders across the stream to form a barrier

Fish are trapped in here

Direction of current

Here's where you probably trapped your finger

Very annoyed fish

## EXERCISE 1.6
### "SURVIVAL PLAN"
### HANDS-ON BOOK P.7
### CREDITS: 2 FOR EACH IDEA

# HOW TO COOK FOOD WITHOUT A KITCHEN

**OK, so you've got your water, and you've caught a fish or snared an animal. How are you going to cook it? (First you've got to prepare it, but since that involves skinning and gutting animals, we'll skip that. I've just had my breakfast, and Mr. Snookums is squeamish.)**

You know how to make a fire, so that's a start. If you've got a mess pan you can simply cook using that. But here are some other ways:

- Skewer the meat on a spit and roast it over embers, or beside a blazing fire. Roast it slowly—roast it too fast and the outside will cook, but the inside may not.
  Good for: meat, poultry
- You can grill your food, but you will need wire mesh to grill on.
  Good for: fish, small pieces of meat, vegetables
- You can wrap food in clay and place it in the embers of the fire. (This is good for fish because when the clay is removed, all the scales go with it. Also good for porcupines – it removes all the spines!
  Good for: fish, porcupine, meat
- If you can find a pot, you can boil water over the flames. Pots can be hung over the fire using a long pole. You can even make a pot hook to allow you to hang the pot at different heights and control the cooking.
  Good for: stews made from small chunks of meat, vegetables

## ROASTING ON A SPIT

The meat should be roasted to one side of a hot fire, allowing the fat to drop into a tray beneath.

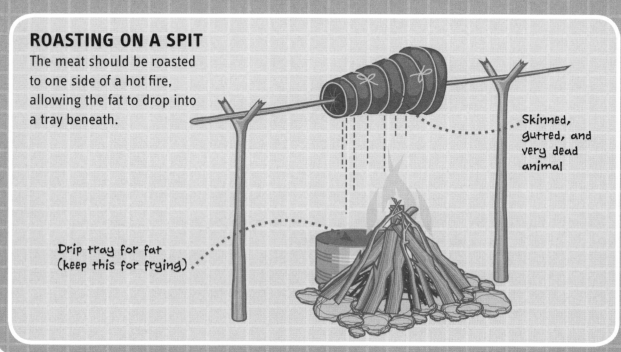

Skinned, gutted, and very dead animal

Drip tray for fat (keep this for frying)

## BOILING

Hang your pot over the fire using a long pole, weighted down by some rocks.

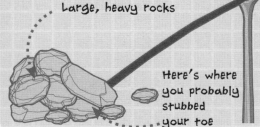

Large, heavy rocks

Cooking pot containing water, food, really annoyed fish, etc.

Here's where you probably stubbed your toe

## POT HOOK

Using a branch with several spurs, you can make a simple pot hook. This allows you to vary the temperature at which you cook your food.

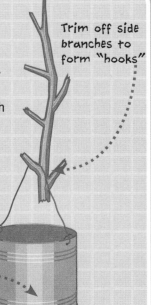

Trim off side branches to form "hooks"

Cooking pot containing water, food, and really, really annoyed fish

VON STRUDELHOPF SAYS, "COOKING FOOD IN SURVIVAL SITUATIONS CAN BE VERY DIFFICULT. I REMEMBER ONCE WHEN I WAS STRANDED ON AN ICEBERG I WAS FACED WITH STARVATION. FORTUNATELY I HAD MY PHONE, SO I WAS ABLE TO ORDER SOME PIZZA. I HAD PIZZA DELIVERED EVERY DAY UNTIL I WAS RESCUED."

# EXERCISE 1.7
## "FOOD TEST"
### HANDS-ON BOOK P.8
### CREDITS: 2 FOR EACH CORRECT ANSWER

# HOW TO MAKE AN EFFICIENT CAMP

**The longer you stay in one place, the more organized you have to be. If there are more than one of you in the survival situation, then organize a rotation for chores. Make sure everyone takes turns at the unpleasant tasks.**

 **WARNING**
NEVER LEAVE THE FIRE UNATTENDED. IF POSSIBLE, MAKE SURE SOMEONE IS IN THE CAMP AT ALL TIMES, IN CASE YOU NEED TO SIGNAL A PASSING AIRCRAFT.

**Some jobs that need doing every day are:**

- collecting firewood
- checking the traps
- hunting or fishing for food
- cleaning the camp
- checking your supplies
- cooking the main meal
- washing the dishes
- maintaining the fire

## CAMP HYGIENE

• Make sure your toilet area is away from the camp and the water supply. Make sure it is downwind as well! If you have a stream nearby, establish a drinking-water point and a washing point, which should be downstream of the drinking-water point.

• Add any trash that can be burned to the fire.

• Gut and clean fish and animals outside the camp. You can do it near a trap—the smell might lure more animals your way.

• Keep your clothes and equipment in a safe, dry place. Make sure they can't get wet or damaged.

RAY DIXON SAYS, "GOOD JOB! YOU SURVIVED THE SURVIVAL SECTION! MORE ADVANCED STUDENTS CAN FIND DETAILS OF ALL MY EXTRA CLASSES ON P.60, AS WELL AS A LIST OF THE EXPEDITIONS YOU CAN GO ON. ALL YOU NEED TO DO NOW IS ADD UP YOUR SCORES FOR THIS SECTION IN THE HANDS-ON BOOK TO SEE IF YOU'VE PASSED!"

P.S. MR. SNOOKUMS SAYS "GOOD JOB" TOO.

## EXERCISE 1.8
"CHORE ROTATION"
HANDS-ON BOOK P.9
CREDITS: 10

# NAVIGATION

Hello! Or as my Viking ancestors would have said, "Kveða!"

For many thousands of years, my people have traveled the globe on voyages of exploration. My ancestor, Sven the Clueless, spent many years of his life sailing the seas—often in circles. He and many others crossed the rolling, storm-tossed seas. They crossed the deathly, white-hot sands. They crossed the road when the little man was flashing white and went shopping. Yes, every day was a voyage for my intrepid ancestors. Now I, Bjorn, son of Sigurd, son of Bjorn, son of Sigurd, son of Doris, son of Sigurd, etc., will take you voyaging. I will train you how to look at the stars. I will train you how to look at the clouds. I will train you how to look at maps. (I will not train you how to bark like a seal, that is Von Strudelhopf's job!)

So lower the plank, and let us board our longship into unknown waters like the brave warriors we are!

Bjorn Sigurdsson

## IN THIS SECTION

1. THE CLIMATE ZONES OF THE WORLD

2. THE (VERY) EXCITING HISTORY OF NAVIGATION

3. HOW TO MAKE YOUR OWN MAPS

4. HOW TO NAVIGATE USING THE STARS

5. HOW TO USE A COMPASS

6. HOW TO "READ" THE CLOUDS

7. MODERN NAVIGATION

# CLIMATE ZONES

**This section gives you an overview of the different climate zones in the world. Why does this matter? Because explorers need to know what weather they will encounter before they sail their longboat into the unknown.**

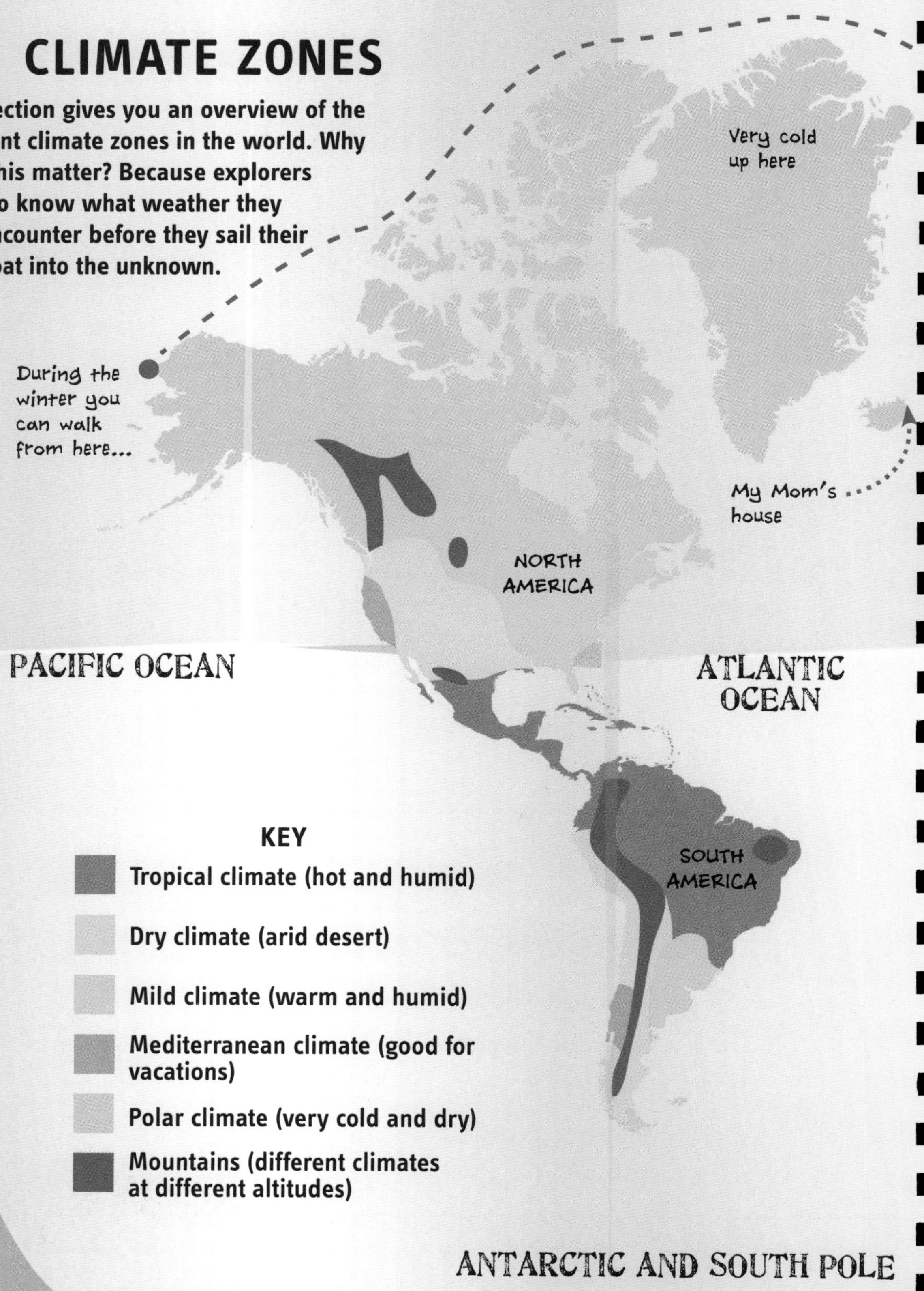

Very cold up here

During the winter you can walk from here...

My Mom's house

NORTH AMERICA

PACIFIC OCEAN

ATLANTIC OCEAN

SOUTH AMERICA

### KEY

Tropical climate (hot and humid)

Dry climate (arid desert)

Mild climate (warm and humid)

Mediterranean climate (good for vacations)

Polar climate (very cold and dry)

Mountains (different climates at different altitudes)

ANTARCTIC AND SOUTH POLE

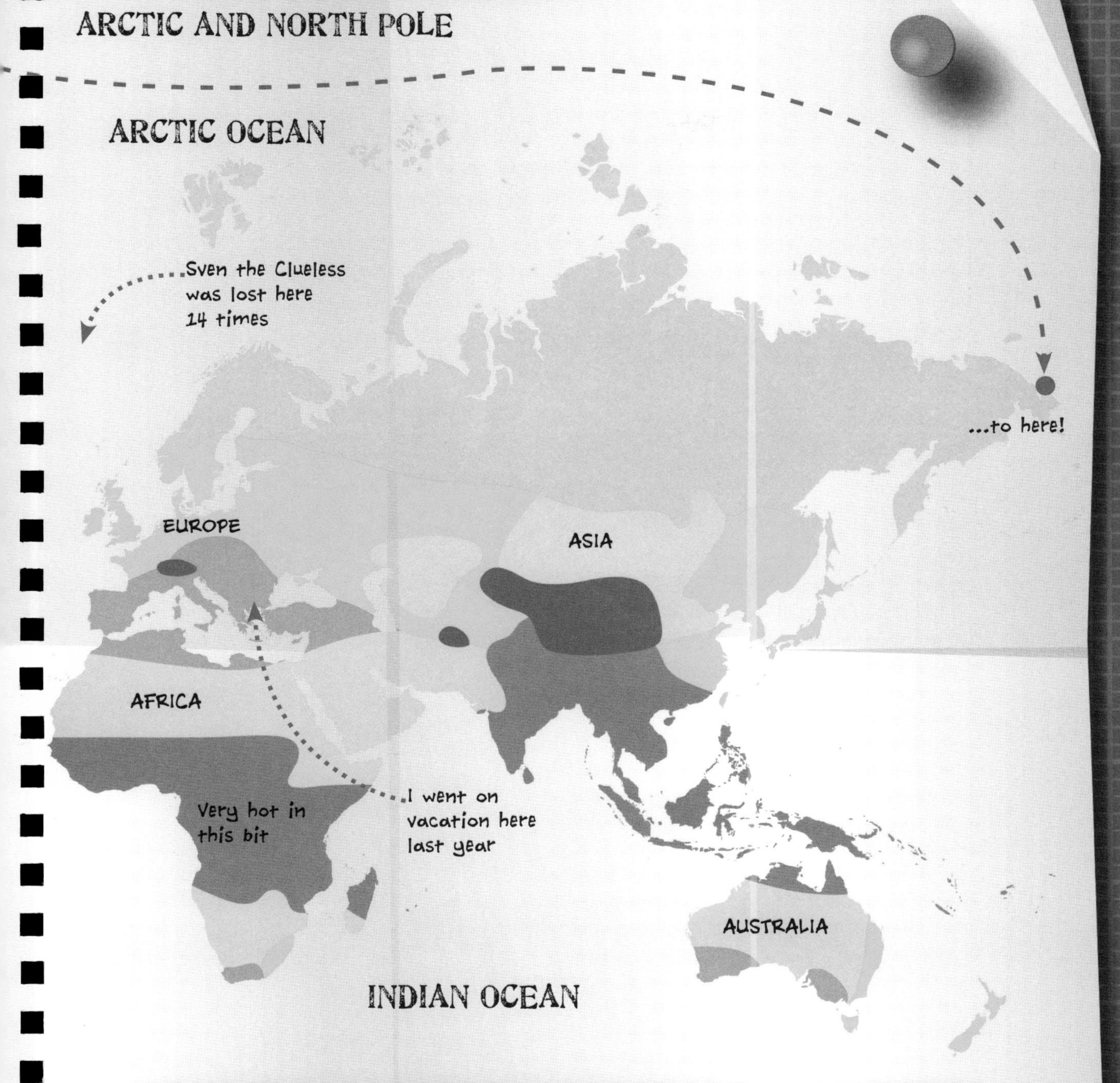

# ARCTIC AND NORTH POLE

## ARCTIC OCEAN

Sven the Clueless
was lost here
14 times

...to here!

EUROPE

ASIA

AFRICA

Very hot in
this bit

I went on
vacation here
last year

AUSTRALIA

## INDIAN OCEAN

## EXERCISE 2.1
"WHAT'S THE CLIMATE?" HANDS-ON BOOK P.12
CREDITS: 10

NAVIGATION

# THE (VERY) EXCITING HISTORY OF NAVIGATION

**Today's explorer can benefit from many great inventions, such as satellite navigation. In previous eras, exploration was a bit harder!**

Nature provided the first explorers with a guide; using their knowledge of weather and tides, they could tell if land was near. Certain types of seabirds might help—for example the frigate bird, which is seen at sea but cannot land on water. When sailors see a frigate bird they know that land cannot be far away.

## COMPASSES

The compass is a crucial tool for explorers. Compasses were not developed until about 1200. They were used on ships to tell sailors which direction they were going. A compass always points to the magnetic north. However, early compasses were not always trustworthy, since the needle can be attracted to other metal objects. So if a compass was put too near iron it would point to that, leading the ship astray.

Needle points to magnetic north

## ASTROLABE

An astrolabe is a device for measuring the height of the sun at noon. This could tell sailors their latitude. The astrolabe is a disc with degrees marked on a circular scale around the edge, and a rotating arm with two eyeholes at either end. The mariner would rotate the arm until the sunlight shone through the two holes. The pointer would then indicate the height of the sun in degrees above the horizon.

Astronomer turns pointer until the sunlight shines through the two eyeholes

Pointer shows the sun's height in degrees measured round the outside.

NAVIGATION

## LATITUDE AND LONGITUDE

Latitude and longitude are imaginary lines running around the earth. They are used to identify your position. Lines of latitude circle the earth from east to west, lines of longitude from north to south. Latitude is measured in degrees, north or south of the equator. The equator is 0°, the North Pole 90° north and the South Pole 90° south. Longitude is also measured in degrees, this time east or west of a line called the prime meridian, which runs through Greenwich, England. (The prime meridian at Greenwich is 0°. If you were at 74° west, you'd probably be in New York. Then you could go shopping.)

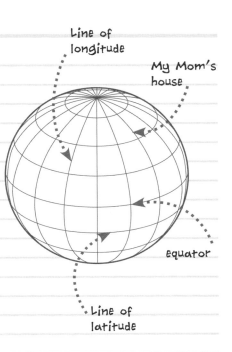

Line of longitude

My Mom's house

equator

Line of latitude

## QUADRANT AND SEXTANT

The quadrant was used to calculate latitude by measuring the height of a star. The navigator looked at the star through two eyeholes and the arm showed the height of the star in degrees, as measured on a scale along the bottom edge. It was superceded by the octant, which used mirrors, and then by the sextant, which was fitted with double mirrors and a telescope for greater accuracy. Often ship's navigators would use these on land rather than onboard ship, since they required a steady hand to be accurate.

Eyeholes

Scale

## EXERCISE:
### "LATITUDE AND LONGITUDE"
### HANDS-ON BOOK P.13 CREDITS: 5

# HOW TO MAKE YOUR OWN MAPS

**Maps are one of the most important tools for any explorer.**
**Maps can show you where you are, where you want to be, and how to get there.**
**Maps can show you how to find vital resources such as water; they can show you hidden**
**dangers such as ravines; they can even show you what's on the bottom of the sea.**

## HEIGHT AND TERRAIN

Maps record the height of the land using contour lines. The height is recorded at 50 ft (50 m) intervals and then the points are connected. The result is something like this:

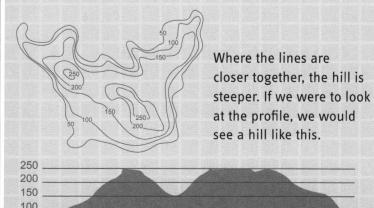

Where the lines are closer together, the hill is steeper. If we were to look at the profile, we would see a hill like this.

## SCALE

All maps have a scale, usually shown by a scale bar. This will show how long a mile or kilometer is on the map. They will also show the ratio. A figure on your map which says, for example, 1:25,000 means that every distance on the map represents a distance that is 25,000 times bigger on the ground.

1 in = 20 mi
1 cm = 13 km               1:1,300,000

```
0          15        30 Miles
0      15      30 Kilometers
```

## FEATURES

Different features on the ground will be shown on the map by different symbols or colors. Rivers are usually blue lines; marshes are often shown as small green tufts of grass, woods as blocks of green. Understanding these will tell you a lot of information about the place you are in.

| | |
|---|---|
| lake | bare rock |
| ponds | open land |
| uncrossable river | partially-open land |
| stream | rough open land |
| narrow marsh | forest: run |
| major ditch | forest: walk |
| uncrossable marsh | forest: impenetrable |
| crossable marsh | built-up areas |
| waterhole | out of bounds |
| well | cultivated land |
| special water feature | orchards |

## GRID REFERENCES

Most maps have a grid, dividing the map into degrees of latitude and longitude (see p.27). Using this grid, you identify your position through a map coordinate. The dot on this grid can be described as 162248. By imagining each square is subdivided into ten smaller units, you can imagine it as 16+2 across and 24+8 up. Of course, today satellite navigation systems can give your precise location, but using map references is a useful skill.

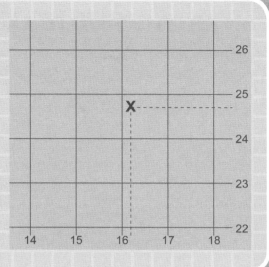

## MAPMAKING

As an explorer you may well go to places that have never been properly mapped. For your own use, and for those who might follow you, you could map the region yourself. Making your own map will help you avoid getting lost. With a map you'll be able to find your way back to camp, and you can mark important areas, like sources of water, areas for hunting, etc.

• Make sure that your map records anything of particular interest, such as unusual rocks, isolated trees, etc.

• You can measure distances by counting your steps.

• You can judge heights by looking at ridges (climb a tree to get a better view).

• You should record the position of important landmarks, such as large trees, rocky outcrops, caves, etc.

• You should record the places where you have set traps to catch animals, or the locations of fish traps on streams.

• You can mark the direction of tracks and paths.

• You can also align your map to the north by using a compass (see p.33).

## EXERCISE 2.3
### "BACKYARD MAP" HANDS-ON BOOK P.14
### CREDITS: 10

# USING THE STARS

**The oldest method of navigating is to follow the stars. My Viking forefathers followed the stars on all their travels, which explains why my ancestor Sven the Clueless kept crashing his boat. It's really difficult sailing in the dark. You can use either the star that's nearest to us (it's that big yellow thing called the Sun) or those that are a long, long way away.**

## USING THE SUN

The sun rises in the east and sets in the west (it's not quite exact—it varies with the season—but it's close enough). So at the very least, you can tell where east, west, north, and south is from the direction of the sunrise. Plants tend to grow towards the sun: in the northern hemisphere they will point more to the south; in the southern hemisphere they will point toward the north. On trees you can check moss; it will be slightly greener and lusher on the "sunny side" of the tree.

## USING THE STARS

For thousands of years travelers have used the stars to give them directions. And those same stars are available to us today. Of course, using the stars is not as accurate as using a compass, or an electronic navigation system, but at least the stars never run out of batteries!

### NORTHERN HEMISPHERE

In the northern hemisphere we use the North Star to orient ourselves. The North Star is the only star that appears not to move. It is located almost directly above polar north.

### Finding the North Star

Finding the North Star is tricky at first. But there are two main ways to find it.

1. From the Big Dipper: The Big Dipper is an easy-to-spot group of stars. If you go to the end and trace a line through two stars Dubhe (A) and Merak (B), they point almost directly to the North Star (C).

2. From Cassiopeia. Cassiopeia is a W-shaped group of stars, on the opposite side of the North Star from the Big Dipper. If you take a line from a star at the end of the W called Chaph (E) to a star in the Big Dipper called Phad (D), it will pass almost straight through the North Star (Polaris).

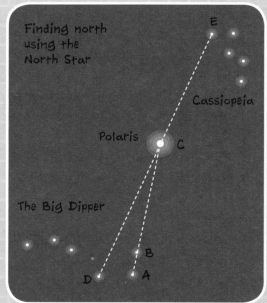

Finding north using the North Star

E

Cassiopeia

Polaris    C

The Big Dipper

B

D    A

## SOUTHERN HEMISPHERE

There is no equivalent of the North Star in the southern hemisphere. Instead, mariners use a pattern of stars called the Southern Cross. This constellation can be distinguished from other cross-shaped constellations by its size and by two pointer stars nearby. To locate south, you have to imagine a line going from Star A through Star B and beyond, about 4.5 times the length. This will give you south.

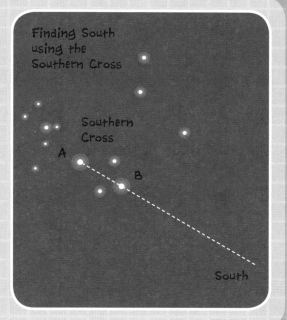

Finding South using the Southern Cross

Southern Cross

A

B

South

## A BIT MORE HISTORY

Humans have used the stars to find their way around since the beginning of recorded history. One of the most ancient accounts of using the stars for navigating is in Virgil's *Aeneid*, written in the first century B.C. There, a ship's navigator, Palinurus, uses stars such as Arcturus, the Great Bear, Hyades, and Orion to plot a course. Among the first navigators to use the stars were Arabic peoples in the desert. Given the desert is full of (a) sand and (b) nothing else, there aren't many landmarks to navigate by. So the people of the desert learned to use the stars, and that's why many of the stars have Arabic names. (For instance, in the diagram opposite, Dubhe comes from the Arab phrase Kahel Ad-Dubb, which means "the back of the bear." Later on, Arabic astronomers wrote books about the stars. The most famous is a book called *The Book of Fixed Stars* by 'Abd Al-Rahman Al Sufi, which was written around 964 A.D.!

## EXERCISE 2.4
### "FIND THE NORTH STAR" HANDS-ON BOOK P.15
### CREDITS: 10

# USING A COMPASS

**A compass is a tool that shows direction. It has a small, magnetized needle that swings, either because it is balanced on a tiny post, or because it is floating on oil or water (sometimes both at the same time). There are several different kinds of compasses, from simple compasses to complicated electronic devices.**

## USING A COMPASS

The compass is the most important navigational tool you have. Here we will look at the basics of using a compass.

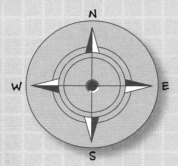

The compass needle always points towards the earth's magnetic north pole. Since the needle has two ends, the end that points to the north is either colored red, or marked with an arrow or a big "N"—something to mark it distinctly.

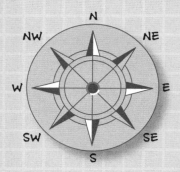

The compass has four main points, or cardinal points. These are North, South, East, and West. If you think of a compass like a clock, the North is at 12, East at 3, South at 6, and West at 9. North and South are easy to remember; East and West can be identified by remembering the word "WE" (West is on the Left and East on the right or the compass face). The intercardinal points are halfway between the cardinal points. They are Northeast, Southeast, Southwest, and Northwest.

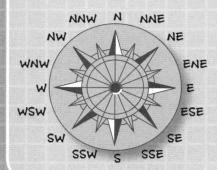

Want more? Well, there are eight more compass points, called the secondary intercardinal points. They lie halfway between the cardinal points (N, S, W, and E) and the intercardinal points (NE, SE, SW, and NW). They are named according to the points they lie between. The cardinal point comes first, and then the intercardinal point.

## USING YOUR COMPASS TO FIND YOUR DIRECTION

Using a compass is very easy if you only want to go north, because that's the way it points! However, what if you want to go west? Here's what you do.

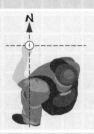

1. Hold your compass flat so that the needle steadily points north.

2. Keeping the compass steadily pointing north, turn to look along the line pointing west. The best way to do this is to hold the compass in your left hand. Turn yourself, don't turn the compass!

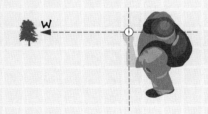

3. Now, looking west, find a landmark that is in that direction—it might be a gate or a tree; just choose something that you can head towards.

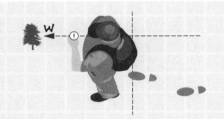

4. Ready, set, go! Head towards the landmark. To avoid getting off course, make sure to look at the compass frequently, say every 328 feet or hundred meters at least. And don't stare at the compass all the time, or else you'll end up walking into a tree!

## EXERCISE 2.5
### "GO NAVIGATE!" HANDS-ON BOOK P.16
### CREDITS: 5-10

# READING THE CLOUDS

**The clouds can tell you what weather is coming so keep your "weather eye" alert! If you learn to recognize clouds, you will be able to navigate your way more safely. If you know a storm is coming, you can seek shelter, rather than be caught in the open. The general rule is: the higher the clouds, the better the weather.**

## Cirrocumulus

Above 18,000 feet. Sometimes they are called a "mackerel" sky, because they look like the stripes on a mackerel. Usually signs of fine weather, they fade quickly after a storm.

## Contrails

These are simply lines left by airplanes.

## Cumulonimbus

From near ground level to over 50,000 feet. Sometimes called "thunderheads," these are huge towering clouds that will bring hail, thunder, lightning, and probably strong winds as well. Not good news.

## Cumulus

Below 6,000 feet. These are fluffy white clouds.
If they are sparsely scattered on the sky, they indicate fair weather, but if they cluster together they can produce sudden showers.

## Fog

Low, dense, airbound sogginess. Best to stay indoors, really.

VON STRUDELHOPF SAYS, "IF YOU SEE CUMULUS CLOUDS IN THE DISTANCE AT SEA, THEY ARE AN INDICATION OF LAND BENEATH THEM. ALWAYS TAKE CARE, HOWEVER. I ONCE SPENT THREE DAYS SAILING TOWARDS SOME CLOUDS IN THE DISTANCE, ONLY TO FIND THAT SOMEONE HAD STUCK SOME COTTON WOOL TO THE END OF MY TELESCOPE."

## Cirrostratus

Anywhere above 18,000 feet.
These thin white clouds are made up of ice particles.
A lot of these in a dark sky means rain is on its way.

## Cirrus

Anywhere above 18,000 feet. Cirrus clouds are thin, wispy clouds that are seen in fine, sunny weather.

## Altostratus

6,000–20,000 feet. These form a kind of gray curtain, dimming the sun. If they start to thicken and darken, rain is coming.

## Nimbostratus

Below 6,500 feet. Dark, gloomy clouds that spread across the sky.
A sign that rain or snow is coming.

## Altocumulus

6,000–20,000 feet. Similar to cirrocumulus but slightly larger, these are signs of fair weather. They usually appear after a storm.

## Statocumulus

Below 6,000 feet. Low, rolling, lumpy clouds that may bring light showers. If these appear in the morning, they often disappear after noon to leave a clear sky.

## Stratus

Below 6,000 feet. The lowest of the clouds, these are "foggy" in appearance, sometimes bringing drizzle.

## EXERCISE 2.6
### "CLOUDWATCHING" HANDS-ON BOOK P.17
### CREDITS: 5

# MODERN NAVIGATION

We have looked at various historical ways of navigating, but the good news is that nowadays a lot of it can be done at the press of a button. Sven the Clueless would have been very happy to have had an electronic Global Positioning System (GPS). (Although he would probably have lost the manual. And his brother, Eric the Very Clumsy, would have sat on the GPS and broke it.)

## MODERN DEVICES

In the electronic age, methods of navigation got easier and easier. The invention of the radio meant that you could get an accurate time check almost anywhere in the world.

At sea, marine radar systems can help identify objects on the seabed and the depth of different sea-lanes or channels.

In recent years, navigation has been revolutionized by satellites and GPS—global positioning systems. Satellite phones keep you in touch wherever you are in the world.

Global positioning systems are handheld electronic devices that give you your exact latitude and longitude at the press of a button. Satellite systems can also give accurate pictures of the earth's surface, meaning that maps are more accurate than ever before.

BJORN SAYS,
"WELL DONE, OH WARRIOR. YOU HAVE MASTERED THE ANCIENT SKILLS OF MY PEOPLE AND THE MORE MODERN SKILLS OF MY PEOPLE WHO NOW HAVE RADAR AND GPS. NOW GO AND EXPLORE, AND MAY YOUR LONGSHIP ALWAYS HEAD IN THE RIGHT DIRECTION!"

VON STRUDELHOPF SAYS, "MODERN DEVICES ARE UNDOUBTEDLY VERY HELPFUL. HOWEVER, THE EXPERIENCED EXPLORER SHOULD NOT RELY TOO HEAVILY ON THESE DEVICES IN CASE THEY BREAK DOWN OR ARE DAMAGED. ON MY LAST EXPEDITION MY SATELLITE PHONE WAS EATEN BY A LARGE PUFFIN. FORTUNATELY, I WAS STILL ABLE TO MAKE CONTACT BY PRESSING THE PUFFIN'S STOMACH AND SPEAKING THROUGH HIS BEAK. THERE ARE MANY ATLASES IN THE MAP ROOM, OF COURSE. AND GLOBES. WHICH ARE NOT TO BE USED AS SOCCER BALLS, REMEMBER."

# HISTORY

What is it that makes people explore? Why do people cross deserts, climb mountains and ford rivers? Is it just to see what's there? Is it because they are bored? Is it because they are holding the map the wrong way around? Whatever the cause, humans have felt the urge to explore for many thousands of years, ever since the first caveman looked out of his cave and said to himself, "I wonder what's over that hill?" (He wouldn't have used these words, obviously. He'd have said something a bit more like "Ugh-ugh-ugh-grunt.")

In this section we will examine some of the history of exploration. And we will look at some of the great explorers; the heroes of exploration, who endured hardship, pain, and really sore feet to find new lands. We'll look at what they were looking for, where they went, and what they did when they got there.

Paolo Marco

## IN THIS SECTION

1. WHY DO PEOPLE EXPLORE?
2. FAMOUS EXPLORERS
3. EXPLORATION AND TRADE
4. HOW TO NAME PLACES YOU DISCOVER
5. LEARNING AND COMMUNICATION

# WHY DO PEOPLE EXPLORE?

**Today exploration is mostly about scientific investigation, but in days gone by there were many reasons why people set out to find new lands.**

## TO FIND LIVING SPACE

People need land to live in. When things got a bit crowded at home, people went to find new places to settle. For example, in 500 B.C. a Phoenician called Hanno led a fleet of ships down the west coast of Africa to establish new colonies. His account records many strange experiences, including meeting "people" who were entirely covered in hair. These were probably chimpanzees (although they may have been prehistoric rock guitarists).

## TO FIND MORE FOOD

Often the urge was simply to find food. The first sea explorers were fishermen, who began to travel further and further afield in order to find new stocks of fish. Some of the earliest trade routes were developed to find salt (see p.44).

## TO MAKE MONEY

Many of the most famous voyages made by explorers came about because people wanted to find valuable items like silk, spices, or gold. These were rare in Europe, sometimes because of growing conditions, sometimes because the Europeans didn't know how to make something (for example travelers to the East often brought back porcelain—a kind of semitransparent pottery that only the Chinese knew how to make). So one of the main reasons people traveled was to come back and make loads of money!

## TO SPREAD THEIR RELIGION

Many voyages of exploration began because people wanted to spread their religion. Today there are things like TV and the Internet, but in those days if you wanted to tell people about your beliefs you had to go and talk to them. The Jesuits (members of a Christian religious order founded in 1540) were active in South America, while St. Francis Xavier was the first European to visit Japan.

## TO DO SCIENTIFIC RESEARCH

In the 18th century, exploration became more concerned with science. Where early explorers wanted to find gold and spices, scientific explorers wanted to find new species of animals and plants. Explorers went to South America and Asia and brought back new specimens of plants, many of which still grow in our gardens today. Perhaps the most famous of the scientific explorers was Charles Darwin, whose trip to the Galapagos Islands and South America led to the theory of evolution. Alexander the Great (356-323 B.C.) went into many new territories in order to build an empire. But he took with him geographers, astronomers, mathemeticians and botanists—the earliest example of scientific exploration.

## BECAUSE THEY WERE WRONG

Many people found new places because they were wrong. Christopher Columbus, for example, believed that if he went far enough west he would discover a new route to China. In fact, to his dying day, he continued to believe it was China he had landed in (rather than America).

## TO SEE WHAT WAS THERE

Have you ever looked over a wall, or run to the top of a hill, just to see what was there? Many explorers have been spurred on by a simple desire to see what's over the next hill. When the famous British mountaineer George Mallory was asked in 1923 why he wanted to climb Mount Everest, he replied, "Because it's there." Sadly, Mallory died on Everest the following year, and his body was not found till May 1999, seventy-five years later.

VON STRUDELHOPF SAYS, "SOMETIMES PEOPLE MAKE GREAT DISCOVERIES BECAUSE THEY ARE LOST. GREENLAND, FOR EXAMPLE, WAS FIRST DISCOVERED BY A NORSEMAN CALLED GUNNBJÖRN, WHO ONLY FOUND THE PLACE BECAUSE HIS SHIP WAS BLOWN OFF COURSE. I HAD THIS EXPERIENCE MYSELF, WHEN SOME YEARS AGO, I WENT TO BUY A PAPER AT THE CORNER STORE. UNFORTUNATELY I TOOK A WRONG TURN AND ENDED UP IN MONGOLIA, WHERE I DISCOVERED THREE NEW VALLEYS AND A LAKE. I NEVER DID GET MY NEWSPAPER."

## EXERCISE 3.1
### "WHY EXPLORE?" HANDS-ON BOOK P.20
### CREDITS: 10+

# FAMOUS EXPLORERS

**Here are just a few of the heroes who have risked their lives to explore new places.**

### ERIK THE RED (AROUND 950–1010 A.D.)

Around 980 a Norse chieftan called Eric Thorvaldsson (known as Erik the Red) killed a man in a quarrel and was forced to flee. Originally he went to Iceland, then he sailed to a land further west. Finding summer grass growing near the landing point, he named the land "Greenland". This was a bit of a mistake, as Greenland is actually colder and icier than Iceland. Still, calling a land "Evencolderandicierland" might not have been very cheerful.

### BJARNI HERJULFSSON AND LEIF ERIKSSON (A LITTLE LATER)

In 986 Bjarni Herjulfsson was on his way to join Erik in Greenland when he was blown off course in a gale. After sailing through banks of fog, he discovered North America—some 500 years before Columbus. On his return, he told Erik the Red about this land. In 1003 Erik's son, Leif Eriksson, led an expedition, building a settlement called Leifsbudir. One of his fellow explorers discovered vines of wild grapes growing, so Leif named the land Vinland or Wineland.

### MARCO POLO (1254–1324)

Marco Polo was a trader whose explorations in Asia lasted 24 years. He became a servant of Kublai Khan, Emperor of China and grandson of the warrior Ghengis Khan. During this time, Marco journeyed throughout China and north into Tibet. He returned to Venice in 1295 and in 1298 was taken prisoner by the Genoese. He told tales of his travels to his cellmate—a man called Rustichello—who wrote it all down (and added some parts of his own).

### IBN BATTUTA (1304–1378)

Ibn Battuta was born in Tangier, on the coast of North Africa. He was one of the greatest travelers ever. His voyages took him to Arabia, through the Sahara Desert, to Egypt, then Jerusalem, across to India, and even as far as China. He traveled the east coast of Africa as far down as Mombasa in Kenya. During his lifetime he traveled around 75,000 miles, pretty impressive for someone whose name means "Son of a Duckling."

### CHRISTOPHER COLUMBUS (1451–1506)

Columbus was born in Genoa, Italy. As the world was round, he thought that you could get to Asia by sailing west, rather than east, so in 1492 he set out, after persuading the King and Queen of Spain to pay for his voyage. When he discovered America—the "New World"—he thought it was part of China. He made four voyages there, without ever realizing it was a totally new continent.

## VASCO DA GAMA (AROUND 1460–1524)

Vasco Da Gama was the first European sailor to reach India by sea (in 1498). Da Gama discovered that the trade in India was controlled by Muslim merchants, and he had very few goods to trade with. He went back to Portugal, equipped a stronger fleet, and returned to take over the Indian Ocean trade by force.

## HENRY HUDSON (DIED 1611)

Henry Hudson tried to find the Northwest Passage—a route to Asia across the top of America. He never found it, but he did find the Hudson River and Hudson Bay, a huge inland sea. Unfortunately, his ship was trapped in the ice and he had to spend the winter in terrible conditions. When the ice melted in the summer, the crew mutinied. They put Hudson, his young son, and seven sailors into a small boat with no oars and left them to die.

## MERIWETHER LEWIS (1774–1809) AND WILLIAM CLARK (1770–1838)

Lewis and Clark were chosen to lead an expedition across America to the Pacific coast. Their journey—up the Missouri from St. Louis—took them into new territories and led to new contact with native tribes. They finally reached the Pacific coast in December 1805, some eighteen months after setting off.

## JAMES COOK (1728–1779)

In the 18th century, Europeans believed that the South Pacific contained a huge continent that joined Australia, New Zealand and the Solomon Islands. James Cook discovered that they were separate lands. On his first voyage he reached Tahiti; his second voyage took him close to Antarctica, and on his third voyage he discovered Hawaii. His crew were the first Europeans to see a kangaroo (which must have really confused them).

VON STRUDELHOPF SAYS, "WHAT CAN WE LEARN FROM THESE STORIES? (APART FROM THE OBVIOUS STUFF, LIKE 'DON'T TRUST SAILORS WHO HAVE BEEN TRAPPED IN ICE' AND 'DON'T NAME YOUR BOY SON OF A DUCKLING') WE CAN LEARN THAT EXPLORATION IS ABOUT HEROISM AND COURAGE. SO MANY EXPLORERS LOST THEIR LIVES ON THEIR JOURNEYS. I, AND ALL THE SCHOOL, SHOULD SALUTE THEIR BRAVERY."

## DAVID LIVINGSTONE (1813–1873)

David Livingstone was the first European to see the Victoria Falls, a vast waterfall in southern Africa. He led expeditions across the Kalahari Desert and to the source of the Zambezi River. He wanted to abolish slavery and to help the African peoples. Eventually he went missing, and an American named Henry Stanley went to find him. When Stanley found Livingstone, he couldn't think of what to say, so he walked up, took off his hat, and said, "Dr. Livingstone, I presume?"

**FAMOUS EXPLORERS**

# MORE FAMOUS EXPLORERS

### RICHARD BURTON (1821–1890)

Burton was a great scholar, a fearless explorer, and an expert swordsman. With John Hanning Speke, he went to Africa to find the source of the Nile River. (It didn't go well: when they arrived at Lake Tanganyika, Burton's legs were paralyzed, and Speke went deaf because a beetle had crawled into his ear. They eventually stopped speaking to each other.) In 1853, he disguised himself as an Arab to visit the Islamic holy city of Mecca—which was forbidden to non-Muslims. Had he been caught he would certainly have been killed.

### ROALD AMUNDSEN (1872–1928)

Amundsen was a Norwegian explorer who led the first expedition to reach the South Pole. He also sailed through the Northwest Passage and located the exact position of magnetic North Pole and explored the Arctic by air. He died in a plane crash while searching for missing polar explorer Umberto Nobile.

### ROBERT SCOTT (1868–1912)

In 1912, "Scott of the Antarctic" set out to race Amundsen to the South Pole. Unfortunately, when his team arrived at the pole, they discovered Amundsen's flag already there. On the 800-mile journey back, they were ravaged by blizzards, causing frostbite and snow blindness. One of them, Titus Oates, realizing he couldn't go on, but knowing the others would not leave him, walked out into the blizzard, uttering the words, "I am just going outside and may be some time." Trapped by blizzards in their tents, Scott and his two remaining companions died. They were just 11 miles from the supply base.

---

*The Academy Times | Saturday May 23 1961*

## News

### AWARD FOR ERNST VON STRUDELHOPF

**Hørdiigørdii, Iceland**

The United Nations have recognized famed polar explorer Ernst Von Strudelhopf by awarding him the "Explorer of the Century" award. "I'm extremely honored and proud," he told reporters. "Although, to be perfectly honest, I am better than anyone else. So nani-nani-ner." News of the award was greeted with joy in his home town of Glutenfrei, Switzerland. His mother said, "I am very proud of him, but not surprised. When he was young he always had his head in an atlas. We gave him a globe as well, but he broke it when he used it as a soccer ball." At the School of Exploration and Survival, where Von Strudelhopf teaches, the staff were reported to be "very proud," although the Librarian was said to be "more interested in the soccer story."

---

### EXERCISE 3.2
### "EXPLORERS WORD SEARCH" HANDS-ON BOOK P.21
### CREDITS: 13

# EXPLORATION AND TRADE

**From the earliest times, exploration was driven by trade. Viking explorers traded honey, tin, wool, fur, leather, and walrus ivory, in return for goods such as silver, silk, spices, wine, jewelry, glass, and pottery. Later on, expeditions to explore the west coast of Africa led to trade in gold and ivory and, soon after, slaves. These trading voyages were often paid for by investors, who could make huge profits. Today, we live in a different world, where this kind of face-to-face trade is not so vital. But here are some of the things that people traded in in the past.**

## GOLD AND SILVER

Gold has been valued since the earliest times, because of its beauty and rarity. Until the 14th century most of the gold in the world came from West Africa. Gold was traded with China for rare luxuries like silk. When Spanish explorers opened up South America, they found not only gold but silver as well, a discovery which led to the beginning of silver mining in Mexico and South America.

## SLAVES

Sadly, slave trading was a big part of exploration. The Vikings bought and sold slaves in Europe, and a lot of exploration in Africa was undertaken because slaves were carried from Africa to Europe and America. Explorers like Livingstone were horrified that the routes they discovered were being used by slave traders.

## FOOD

Columbus's voyage to the New World led to the discovery of new food products like cocoa, corn, tomatoes, and potatoes, which enhanced the European diet. Europeans also discovered tobacco, which formed a major part of the cross-Atlantic trade for many centuries.

HOW DOES TRADE WORK? TRADE IS EXCHANGING ONE TYPE OF GOODS FOR ANOTHER. FOR EXAMPLE, YOU MIGHT NOT HAVE MUCH TIMBER, BUT YOU PRODUCE METAL. SO WHAT DO YOU DO? YOU MAKE THE METAL INTO AXES, TRAVEL TO A FOREST, AND TRADE THE AXES WITH WOODCUTTERS FOR LOTS AND LOTS OF WOOD. THEY NEED THE AXES, YOU NEED THE WOOD: EVERYONE'S HAPPY.

## LUXURY GOODS

From the East came precious gems and fine silk. The route to China to get these goods (known as the Silk Road) was dangerous and difficult, and you couldn't carry very much when traveling overland. So traders started looking for sea routes. Using the sea you could fill several ships with goods, and there were fewer enemies to get in the way.

**TRADE**

## SPICES

It might surprise you to know that spices have inspired more exploration than virtually any other item. European food in the Middle Ages was not very tasty. They didn't have any refrigerators to keep their meat fresh. What they needed was a bit of spice. And spices came from a long way away. The demand for spice, and the difficulty of obtaining it, made spices very valuable. You could pay people in spice. Spices could also be used to pay fines and mortgages, to buy land, to buy a coat of arms, or to pay taxes.

## SALT

Salt is widely available today, but at one point it was so valuable that people were paid in it (which is the origin of the word "salary"). In an age before refrigerators and freezers, salt was vital not only for flavoring food, but also for preserving it.

## NUTMEG

Nutmeg originally came from the Banda Islands (part of Indonesia). In Elizabethan times it was believed that nutmeg could ward off the plague, so the spice was very popular.

## PEPPER

Pepper was farmed all over southern Asia more than 2,000 years ago. Pepper was so precious that, at times, it was used as money. Pepper was used extensively in cooking, but could also be used as an insect repellent!

## CINNAMON

Cinnamon was at one time more valuable than gold. It comes from the bark of the cinnamon tree, which grows in Sri Lanka, the West Indies, and Brazil. It was not only used for food, but also in cosmetics, drugs, and perfume.

## CLOVES

Cloves came from the Maluku Islands (south of Indonesia), which became known as the Spice Islands. Cloves were incredibly valuable—2 lb cost around ($\frac{1}{4}$ oz) of gold; that's around $178 at today's prices!

### EXERCISE 3.3
#### "TRADE QUIZ"  HANDS-ON BOOK P.22
#### CREDITS: 10

# HOW TO NAME THE PLACES YOU DISCOVER

**Imagine the scene: you find a new island, uncharted, not on any known map. After first checking that it's safe to land and you won't get (a) eaten by savage animals, (b) swallowed up by quicksand or (c) attacked by the local tribesmen, you will have to find a name for the place.**

In the old days it was easy: simply pick the name of your ruler or monarch, or the person who paid for the expedition and use that. (That's why there are so many places around the world called "Victoria Something"—because most of these were discovered during the reign of Queen Victoria.)

Now, however, it's a bit more complicated. Fewer countries have kings or queens, and you can't name a place after a president or prime minister because they change too often. You could name it after the person who funded your expedition, but in these days of sponsorship deals you might find yourself declaring, "I name this land 'Roy's Used Truckstop-Island'" or something like that.

Also, you should be sure that you really are the first to discover it. Livingstone was the first European to see the Victoria Falls, but others had already noticed them—hardly surprising, given that they are 350 ft (108 meters) high and 5,500 ft (1700 meters) wide. Local tribes already had a name for them: "Mosi-oa-tunya" or "the Smoke that Thunders."

VON STRUDELHOPF SAYS, "PROBABLY THE BEST BET IS SIMPLY TO NAME THE LAND AFTER YOURSELF. I MYSELF HAVE DONE THIS SEVERAL TIMES. ERNST ISLAND IS A SMALL ISLAND SOMEWHERE IN THE ARCTIC; I HAVE SO FAR DISCOVERED MOUNT VON STRUDELHOPF, VON STRUDELHOPF VALLEY AND THE RIVER STRUDELHOPF. I AM CURRENTLY ATTEMPTING TO FOUND A COMPLETELY NEW COUNTRY CALLED ERNSTOPIA, BUT AT THE MOMENT OUR ENTIRE TERRITORY IS LIMITED TO MY GREENHOUSE AND A BIT OF LAND THAT RUNS BEHIND THE GARDEN SHED."

## EXERCISE 3.4
### "NAME THAT PLACE"
### HANDS-ON BOOK P.23
### CREDITS: 10

Land here

Mount Von Strudelhopf

Von Strudelhopf Valley

River Von Strudelhopf

Greenhouse

ERNSTOPIA

border

# LEARNING AND COMMUNICATION

**The most successful explorers are those who learn from the local people, who adopt their customs, and take on their survival tips.**

For example, back in 1535, a French explorer named Jacques Cartier and his men were exploring Canada. At that time, sailing long distances meant having to drink rancid water while eating wormy food and stale biscuits. This horrible diet meant that Cartier and his men caught scurvy (a disease caused by lack of vitamin C), their teeth fell out, and they were too weak to walk. Fortunately some Quebec natives came to their rescue. They made a tea from pine needles, which are high in vitamin C. Cartier and his men were saved by local knowledge, not by their own devices.

## BUT HOW DO YOU TALK TO THEM?

Well, you have to learn their language. One way is to use a picture dictionary. Take with you a photo album containing pictures of objects you might need. That way, if you don't know the words for things, you can point to the pictures and be understood. In fact, this is a good idea even for traveling on vacation.

## HERE ARE SOME THINGS YOU COULD INCLUDE:

- Water, food, your tent
- Objects that you might need (e.g., compass, water bottle, sleeping bag)
- You and your family
- Your home and your town
- Your favorite food
- Various medical supplies
- Different types of transportation

VON STRUDELHOPF SAYS, "BE CAREFUL USING SIGNS AND GESTURES. DIFFERENT SIGNS HAVE DIFFERENT MEANINGS DEPENDING ON WHERE YOU ARE IN THE WORLD. I ONCE WAVED 'HELLO' TO A SHEPHERD IN A REMOTE MOUNTAIN VALLEY, ONLY TO FIND OUT LATER THAT IN HIS LANGUAGE A WAVE MEANS 'PLEASE LET ME MARRY YOUR GREAT-AUNTIE.' LUCKILY I ESCAPED BECAUSE I COULD RUN A BIT FASTER THAN SHE COULD."

PAOLO MARCO SAYS, "WELL DONE. YOU HAVE STARTED TO LEARN ABOUT THE HISTORY OF EXPLORATION. BEAR IN MIND THE COURAGE OF THESE EARLY EXPLORERS AS YOU SET FORTH ON YOUR JOURNEY. LEARN FROM THEM. COPY THEM. ONLY TRY NOT TO END UP LIKE THE DEAD ONES."

## EXERCISE 3.5
### "PICTURE DICTIONARY"
### HANDS-ON BOOK P.24
### CREDITS: 15

# GADGETS AND EQUIPMENT

Hi! Welcome to the Gadgets and Equipment section. This part will tell you more about the equipment you really need to have and some cool gadgets to make exploration easier and more fun. I've spent many years trying out these gadgets (well, not that many years—I'm only 11. But I work fast!) Here's a bit of advice at the start, though—let the expedition decide the gadgets, not the other way round. What I mean is, think about where you're going and plan your trip, then decide what gadgets you need. No point taking a satellite phone if you only need a cell. No point taking a team of huskies if you're going to the desert. Ask yourself, what kind of trip am I going on? How long will I be traveling? What will the weather be like? Take the right equipment for the task and you'll travel better. Have fun.

*Billy MacMasters*

**Billy MacMasters (Lt. Colonel)**

## IN THIS SECTION

1. **HOW TO CHOOSE A BACKPACK**

2. **SELECTING THE BEST CLOTHING**

3. **KNIVES AND TOOLS**

4. **ULTRA-COOL ELECTRONIC GADGETS**

5. **TENTS AND SLEEPING BAGS**

6. **TRANSPORT FOR EXPLORERS**

7. **WHAT TO EAT**

# HOW TO CHOOSE A BACKPACK

Your backpack must be strong, light, and, most of all, comfortable. Before you choose it, make a list of what you're going to put into it for your expedition. You want a pack that is big enough to carry your load but no bigger. Backpacks are normally sized in cubic units—that's how much they can hold. Small packs (called daypacks) start at around 1,800 cubic inches to 2,000 cubic inches. A normal expedition backpack can be over 5,000 cubic inches and can carry up to 80 lb. But if you're a kid like me, you want something a little smaller, otherwise the pack will be bigger than you are!

## FITTING

It's really important that your pack fits, because it will be on your back for a looooong time. So give it a good test. You need a pack with good shoulder straps with plenty of padding. It should also have a wide hip belt—this is going to take most of the load, so make sure it works. Some packs come with side compression straps that help squish all the stuff down a bit. If you can, fill it up with some stuff and run around a bit. Concentrate. Pick up on any minor niggles or problems—these may not seem so bad, but imagine what you'll be feeling after a long day's walk through the jungle! One good thing to look for is whether the backpack allows air to flow between your back and the backpack. This will make life cooler.

## EXTRAS

Make sure your pack has some pockets as well. I've never found a pack—or a pair of trousers—with too many pockets for all my gadgets! (But then I am Gadget Boy!) Plenty of pockets means that you can be really organized about where you stash your stuff. (Not to mention allowing you to keep your smelly pants away from your water bottle!)

Padded shoulder-straps

Top section fully covers top of bag

External pockets for small items that you will need during the day

Separate lower compartment— good for sleeping bags, clothes, etc.

Side compression straps

Straps to secure ice-pick, tools, etc.

Wide, well padded hip belt

## LEARN HOW TO PACK IT

If you're going somewhere where you're going to get wet, then use polythene bags or dry bags. Order is important. Pack your sleeping bag at the bottom and your tent at the top. After all, that's the first thing you're going to need to put up. Put items you need to have handy in side pockets (e.g., maps, medical kit, drinks, stove, etc.).

This shows how the bag should fit the spine. Generally, explorers are not transparent.

Place medium-weight/bulkier items toward the top or down the front of the pack

Heavy items (e.g. water, food, climbing gear, tent, etc.) should go closest to your back. The tent should be at the top

Light items at the bottom, like sleeping bags, etc.

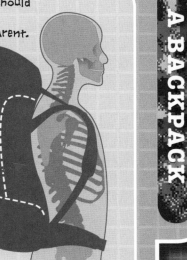

## A REALLY USEFUL GADGET

I'm going to introduce you to one of the simplest and most useful of all gadgets. It's a ziplock bag. (Who said gadgets had to be electrical?) These are the best thing for travelers and explorers. You buy them in packs of 25 or 50 and use them to store all kinds of things—anything from batteries to oatmeal to your dirty socks! They'll keep things sorted and dry.

Ziplocks! You can put (almost) anything in here!

### EXERCISE 4.1
"GET PACKING!"
HANDS-ON BOOK P.28
CREDITS: 10

VON STRUDELHOPF SAYS, "DISORGANIZATION CAN SPELL DISASTER. I ONCE FELL INTO A CREVICE AND, BARELY CONSCIOUS, REACHED FOR MY MEDICAL KIT. IMAGINE MY HORROR WHEN I FOUND, NOT BANDAGES, BUT A PACKET OF KIPPERBUNG'S 'HARD AS A ROCK' DIGESTIVE BISCUITS. FORTUNATELY, BEING KIPPERBUNG'S THEY WERE IN FACT EXTREMELY SOFT AND ABSORBENT, SO I WAS ABLE TO USE THEM AS A KIND OF SPONGE TO STOP THE BLEEDING. EVEN SO, IT WAS A HORRIBLE SITUATION."

# SELECTING THE BEST CLOTHING

**Remember what I said at the beginning? About your expedition deciding the equipment? Well, that's never more true than when it comes to clothing. Think where you're going—then choose the clothing you need.**

## ON YOUR BODY

Clothing should fit well but not be too tight. Always carry with you a set of good rain gear and a sweater or other spare warm clothing, and if the climate is likely to be cold, a warm hat and a pair of gloves. Make use of materials like Gore-Tex™, which is waterproof and breathable. (Hint: keep it clean, though. The fabric can't "breathe" if it's covered in dirt.) Fleece is a synthetic material that is good for insulation. If you get a fleece jacket, find one that's windproof. Wool is still a good, traditional choice; it stays warm even if it gets wet. However, if it does get wet it gets heavy.

## ON YOUR FEET

Your boots and socks are some of the most crucial parts. Get these wrong and you'll regret it. Again, think what you'll be walking on. On mountains you'll need good tough boots. In the tropics you might need a more lightweight pair. In polar conditions, you'll be best with boots made of artificial materials. (And you'll want not only boots, but snowshoes and skis.) And always take a spare pair of laces for your walking boots!

## ON YOUR HEAD

At the other end of your body, you'll need something for your head! Hats will protect you from both heat and cold. In hot temperatures, a hat will provide shade; in cold temperatures, it will prevent you from losing heat from your head. (Did you know that you can lose anything from 30 to 50% of your total body temperature through your head?) In some countries, you are required to cover your head if you are entering a sacred place.

## OVER YOUR EYES

You need sunglasses in hot countries—and in very cold ones as well! Sunglasses protect your eyes from the glare of the sun and also from reflected sunlight on snow-covered landscapes.

## CLOTHING FOR DIFFERENT CLIMATES

The most important thing is to find stuff that is going to protect you from the elements, whether we're talking sun, snow, rain, or wind. As the old saying goes, "There's no such thing as bad weather. Only bad clothing."

## COLD CLIMATES

The important thing here is layering. Rather than one humongous layer, you want lots of separate layers that you can put on and off as required. Some polar explorers find that, if they're pulling sleds or skiing, they don't need several layers.

## HOT CLIMATES

It can be difficult to choose the right clothing for these places. Again, the activity needs to dictate what you wear. On the move you won't need to or want to wear much. Avoid walking in waterproof rain gear because your sweat will condense inside. Cotton is good, because it draws up the sweat away from your body (it's called "wicking"). Wear a hat to protect against sunstroke.

## EXERCISE 4.2
### "THE GREAT BIG GADGET QUIZ"
### HANDS-ON BOOK P.29
### CREDITS: 30

# KNIVES AND TOOLS

**Your knife is your friend. Not literally, obviously. I mean it won't take you out to the movies or remember your birthday—but it will help you survive. And the longer you have it, the more you learn to trust it.**

## MULTIBLADED TOOLS

These can be incredibly useful, offering a variety of tools in one gadget. Normally they come with two blades, a corkscrew, a small saw, screwdrivers, a can opener, and a bottle opener. You can also get bigger ones, with magnifying glass, compass, etc. Avoid the very biggest ones—these look great in the stores, but they're heavy to carry around.

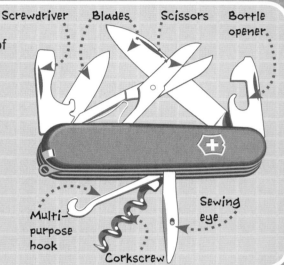

Screwdriver · Blades · Scissors · Bottle opener · Multi-purpose hook · Corkscrew · Sewing eye

## EXTRA TOOLS

Another good tool is a combination folding shovel/pickax. Made out of lightweight metal, these can be used to dig ditches, toilets, etc. You can also get combination tools with an axe on them—good for chopping wood for fire or shelter.

## WARNING
**BEFORE USING A KNIFE, PLEASE GET PERMISSION FROM YOUR HOME TUTOR.**

VON STRUDELHOPF SAYS, "KNIVES ARE DANGEROUS. BUT THE MOST DANGEROUS PART OF THE KNIFE IS THE PERSON CARRYING IT. KNIVES ARE NOT TOYS AND YOU ARE EXPLORERS NOT GANGSTERS. IF YOU CAN'T HANDLE YOUR KNIFE SENSIBLY, THERE IS NO ROOM FOR YOU IN THIS SCHOOL. NEVER CARRY A KNIFE AROUND WITH YOU WHILE YOU'RE OUT ON THE STREETS. AND NEVER TRY TO TAKE ONE IN YOUR CARRY-ON LUGGAGE AT AIRPORTS."

## TOP TIP

"WHEN YOU ARE WALKING THROUGH AREAS WHERE THERE ARE MANY BUSHES OR A LOT OF FOLIAGE (OFTEN TERMED "CLOSE COUNTRY"), MAKE A HABIT OF CHECKING YOUR POSSESSIONS. CHECK YOUR KNIFE AND WATER BOTTLE MOST OF ALL. LOSE THESE AND YOU REALLY ARE IN TROUBLE."

# ULTRACOOL ELECTRONIC GADGETS

**These are so cool, they're subzero! Remember your history lesson in Bjorn's class?
All that stuff about sextants and quadrants and all that?
Well, welcome to the 21st century!**

GADGETS

## GPS (GLOBAL POSITIONING SYSTEMS)

GPS receive radio signals from satellites to give you an exact position, almost anywhere in the world. You can get your position quickly and easily. They come in many shapes and sizes, from handheld ones to the satnav stuff in cars. You can even get them built into watches or cell phones! Some handheld GPS receivers have color screens, but most are black and white. Some come with built-in cool stuff like digital compasses, barometers, waypoint markers, and maps. They need a power supply and you have to take good care of them. So don't rely too much on these dudes. Make sure you know the basics of navigation—like reading a map.

## SATELLITE PHONE

Another cool device for the intrepid explorer. If you're going really wild – like the Arctic or the Sahara, you won't find cell phone reception out there. That's where the satellite phone comes in. A satellite phone uses orbiting satellites to connect with main phone lines; they will work just about anywhere on the planet. You use it like an ordinary phone – just turn it on and dial the number. But they're expensive (anything from $295-$1,500 for the phone and then a lot per minute). And you do need a good view of the sky to operate them.

## CELL PHONE

These are great for trainee explorers, because they mean that you can keep in touch with people. But you may not always get a signal (even in countries like the UK and USA where there are a lot of cell phones, there are also many areas where you can't get a signal.) Also, you've got to have a way of charging the battery. And keeping them dry.

## SOLAR PANELS

With all these electrical gadgets, you need a way of charging them. You can use a solar panel to recharge small items like cell phones etc. Obviously you'll need some sunlight, but it does mean you don't have to carry loads of batteries around with you.

## ALTIMETERS

Going up a mountain? An altimeter is a good idea because it tells you how high you are, and therefore how much further it is to the summit.

There is so much good equipment out there, but the one thing you really need is your brain. Nothing here is a replacement for the ability to think calmly and quickly—and to improvise should you need to.

# TENTS AND SLEEPING BAGS

You'll need some kind of shelter. Of course, you can build your own from scratch (see pp. 12-13) but I think it's easier to take a tent with you! Once again, what you need will be decided by where you're going and what the weather conditions will be like. It's best to keep your tent as light as possible, although if you are traveling in a group, the weight can be shared by splitting the tent up into flysheet, inner, poles, etc.

## TROPICAL TRAVEL

In jungle and hot climates, you need a tent that keeps out the insects and mosquitoes. But it doesn't have to give a great deal of warmth. You can get by without a "proper" tent at all, by using a survival hammock with built-in mosquito netting, which you suspend between two trees.

## POLAR TRAVEL

For cold climates you want a tent that offers plenty of warmth—and also a tent that can be put up quickly in a gale. Polar tents come with insulating outer tents that are tough—and usually brightly colored so that they are highly visible against the white snow. There should also be an inner lining with plenty of space to provide insulation between the two layers.

## DIFFERENT TYPES OF TENTS

**Dome tents** are really aerodynamic and can be put up quickly. Conical tents have traditionally been used by natives of cold climates (such as the Chuchis, Sami, Cree, Naskapi, and Inuit); the dome is the ideal shape to combat intense winds and heavy snow loads. It's also easy to heat.

Dome tent.
Easy to put up,
light to carry

Sloping sides make for good wind- and rain-resistance.

**The wedge or ridge tent** consists of material hung over a ridge pole, to form a kind of upside-down V shape. It's good for trips on which you move a lot because you can put it up quickly and efficiently.

Wedge or ridge tent. It's very simple – you can even make your own tent poles from branches

**Wall tents** are used where you can set up a more permanent camp. They allow people to stand up, providing more space for movement and living. They have a long history of usage—dating back at least 500 years—so they must be a pretty good design!

Side-wall tent. More height, more living space, but not very transportable. Good for a base camp setup.

## SLEEPING BAGS

All explorers need to get plenty of sleep! When choosing a sleeping bag, the first consideration should be warmth, and then weight. Mountaineers need a warmer sleeping bag, for example, but warmer bags weigh more. Bags are generally rated in seasons; from two- to four-season. A four-season bag can be used all year-round. A good idea is to get a bag rated to 10 degrees below the expected temperature for your trip; then, even if it is unexpectedly cold, you'll still be OK.

## INFLATABLE MATTRESSES

To go with your bag, an inflatable mattress is a good idea. These are self-inflating mats that provide an insulating layer between your body and the ground. All you have to do is roll them out on the floor and then open a valve; the valve allows air in to inflate the mattress. When the mattress is full, tighten the valve again, and you have a comfortable night's sleep.

## MOSQUITO NETS

Going to a hot or tropical country? Heading into the jungle or the rain forest? Then you'll need a mosquito net. These are inner tents of fine mesh that cover your bed: you can breathe and stay cool, but the skeeters can't get in.

## EXERCISE 4.2
### "THE GREAT BIG GADGET QUIZ"
### HANDS-ON BOOK P.29
### CREDITS: 30

# TRANSPORTATION FOR EXPLORERS

**Wherever you're going, you'll need a way of getting there! Obviously there are the two parts at the bottom of your legs, but these may not be enough in all circumstances. So here are some other really cool ways of getting around.**

## BY AIR

A plane will get you a long way fast. But flying over something isn't really exploring it in my book. Still for some areas of the world the only way in is to fly there, either by plane or by helicopter. Or air balloon. Some explorers have also used lightweight aircraft, like micro-gliders, for reconnaissance trips.

## BY SEA

Boats are great ways of exploring. (Although not so good on land.) If you're going to the polar regions, you'll need a boat called an ice-cutter, which has specially strengthened hulls. For traveling upriver, you need boats that are light but tough, so that you can carry them over any rapids should you need to. Canoes and kayaks can also come in handy.

## UNDER SEA

Then there's the bottom of the ocean: one of the last truly unexplored places on earth. For this you'll need a submarine called a deep-ocean submersible, which can withstand the huge pressure of water found at the bottom of the ocean. Because there is no light in the deep, the submersible must carry lights to illuminate the seafloor. There's no toilet either, so make sure you go before they shut the hatch.

Deep-ocean submersible

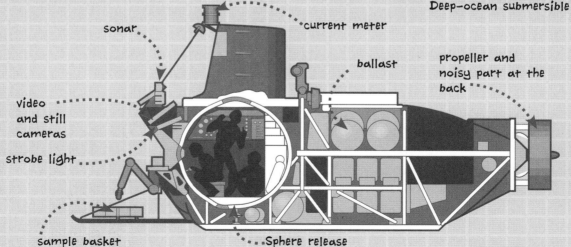

sonar

current meter

ballast

propeller and noisy part at the back

video and still cameras

strobe light

sample basket

Sphere release

The Academy Times | Wednesday August 23 1972 P3

## News

# VON STRUDELHOPF IN CAMEL RESCUE DRAMA

**Veriparkii, Lapland**

Veteran explorer Ernst Von Strudelhopf has failed in his epic attempt to become the first man to reach the North Pole on camel. "I thought it worth a try," he told reporters, "if only to give the camels a change of scenery from all that sand. Sadly, they didn't seem that keen on the snow, either." There were rumors that the explorer only went on the trip to escape a fight at the Amazing Academy School of Exploration and Survival, where he has been accused of causing damage to a highly valuable globe. "I deny it was my footprint found on the globe," he said. "I was nowhere near the library at the time. It must have been someone else with a footprint just like mine. Now please go away – the camel needs a warm bath."

## TRANSPORT

## CARS

Not great for exploration, really, as they need too flat a surface. However, for desert areas and some rough terrain you can use 4x4 vehicles. And you'll need one to get you to the airport. (Or you could take the bus.)

## ANIMALS

Going to the poles? The traditional way is to use a dogsled—a sled pulled by huskies, specifically bred to cope with the cold. Through the desert there are camels, of course; elsewhere ponies and mules are useful.

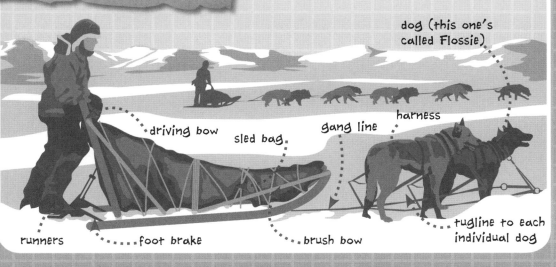

dog (this one's called Flossie)

driving bow

sled bag

gang line

harness

runners          foot brake          brush bow

tugline to each individual dog

# EXERCISE 4.3
## "DESIGN YOUR VEHICLE"
## HANDS-ON BOOK P.31
## CREDITS: 10

# WHAT TO EAT

Where we go there aren't many burger joints or pizza restaurants. So what should you take with you? There is a wide variety of food especially for explorers: precooked meals that have been vacuum-sealed in pouches. All you have to do is open the pouch and cook it. (You don't even need to heat it up, but cold hot dogs and beans are not very appetizing.) However, they're expensive. You can take your own food.

## GOOD FOODS TO CARRY WITH YOU

- Dried meat strips (sometimes called "jerky")
- Cheese—especially the type sealed in wax
- Chocolate (high in energy, but don't take it anywhere hot—it'll melt!)
- Energy food bars, e.g., cereal breakfast bars
- Oatmeal—it weighs hardly anything, and you can cook it fast.
- Rice is quite good, because it swells as it cooks, so you can get several portions out of one packet. (Noodles or couscous are also good if you prefer. They are easy to cook and very light to carry)
- Tea bags or other hot drink mixes. Chances are you'll need warming up at some point!
- Powdered soup
- Jam or peanut butter. Don't take the jar—put some in a ziplock bag, then you can squeeze it out.

VON STRUDELHOPF SAYS, "OF COURSE, YOU CAN ALSO FISH, HUNT, AND EAT LOCAL FOOD. HOWEVER, EVERY EXPLORER, HOWEVER HARDY, NEEDS A BIT OF COMFORT FOOD. I ALWAYS TAKE WITH ME A LARGE FRUITCAKE BAKED BY MY WIFE. IT TASTES APPALLING, BUT IT LASTS FOR WEEKS AND IT REMINDS ME OF WHY I PREFER TRAVELING TO BEING AT HOME. ALSO, IN A TOUGH SPOT YOU CAN THROW IT AT ATTACKING POLAR BEARS."

Instead of carrying food in its original container, you can carry one-portion sized amounts in sealed bags. Then, when you've used the food, you can keep the bag and reuse it.

BILLY MACMASTERS SAYS, "COOL! YOU'VE REACHED THE END OF THE GADGETS STUFF. BUT REMEMBER ANY GADGET IS ONLY AS GOOD AS THE PERSON OPERATING IT. SO MAKE SURE YOUR BRAIN IS SWITCHED ON AS WELL."

## WHAT TO COOK IT ON

You can always make a fire (see p.14) but most travelers take a stove with them. Most camp stoves rely on gas cannisters—if you're going somewhere wild, you aren't going to find a camping store to supply you with spares, so you may need to use solid fuel stoves.

# ADDITIONAL INFORMATION

## IN THIS SECTION...

- SPECIAL COURSES
- GUEST LECTURES
- ANNUAL BANQUET AND AWARDS CEREMONY
- EXPLORERS' EQUIPMENT EMPORIUM
- SCHOOL OF EXPLORATION CLUBS AND SOCIETIES

LOST!
ONE VERY DENTED GLOBE. COULD BE MISTAKEN FOR A SOCCER BALL.

IF FOUND, PLEASE CONTACT THE LIBRARIAN IMMEDIATELY.

AMAZING ACADEMY.
SURVIVAL
UNIQUE ID NUMBER
7MBIC6666
Name Billy MacMan

FOUND!
IS THIS YOURS?
IF SO, PLEASE KEEP IT SAFE NEXT TIME!

**EXTRAS**

# SPECIAL COURSES

In addition to the basic course offered here, students at the Academy can sign up for a number of additional courses that might be of interest. Some of these are run in conjunction with other Amazing Academy schools.

## STUDY WEEK: POLAR SURVIVAL

Led by Professor Von Strudelhopf and with the expert assistance of Ray "Wildman" Dixon, this is a chance for some handpicked students to spend six days getting very, very cold. The course takes place in the Amazing Academy Polar Studies Department, and we will be exploring the high mountain range that borders the Amazing Academy campus on the northeast. Students should be aware that there is a chance of frostbite and snowblindness, although Professor Von Strudelhopf assures us that "We haven't had anyone die. At least not recently."

## SUMMER EXPEDITION: JUNGLE EXPLORATION

In association with the Amazing Academy School of Treasure-Hunting and the School of Jungle Studies, we will be mounting an expedition to explore the tropical jungle on the southeast of the Amazing Academy campus. Students are advised to bring insect repellent. Lots of it. This year we will be attempting to find the Sacred Temple of Quocacuola, with its reputed statues of gold, silver and, unusually, chocolate.

## INDIVIDUAL STUDY WEEK: DESERT ISLAND SURVIVAL WITH UNDERSEA TRIP

Each student is expected to spend one week surviving on the Amazing Academy Desert Island. The week includes a trip on the submersible deep-sea unit from the School of Underwater Adventure. Not recommended for anyone who gets seasick.

**EXTRAS**

# GUEST LECTURES

**During the year we will have a series of guest lectures by distinguished explorers and travelers. Previous lectures have included:**

**HENRY "ARIZONA" SMITH:** How I was grabbed by the Incas and lived to tell the tale.

**ACHMED OF FAA:** Sandstorms I Have Known (illustrated with photos and drawings. Not to mention quite a lot of sand, which he hadn't entirely removed from his robes.)

**BOROMIR KIPPERBUNG:** Supplies and Equipment for Today's Explorer (also illustrated with photos, although, true to form, they proved to be photos of Kipperbung's Garden Furniture Department)

# ANNUAL BANQUET AND AWARDS CEREMONY

**This is a highlight of the year. The banquet traditionally serves a variety of food that has been caught or foraged by students on the course. A typical menu includes edible fungi, seaweed, clay-roasted porcupine, coconuts, and home-brewed root beer served in a cactus shell.**

**The awards covers the following categories:**

- Best Explorer
- Hardiest Survivor
- Most Courageous Student
- Student who has survived biggest fall down a ravine or crevice
- Student who has survived fiercest attack by large predator
- Student who has survived fiercest attack by large predator followed by a fall down ravine/crevice
- Best discovery of the year (this will be awarded in three categories: rivers, mountains, forgotten temples).

Last year's "Best Explorer" winner is presented with his prize by the famous Underwater Explorer Jacques Soufle.

# EXPLORERS' EQUIPMENT EMPORIUM

The Amazing Academy Explorers' Equipment Emporium contains an extensive—and some would say eccentric—range of equipment. Located on the first floor, at the back, behind the training room, it's not easy to find, but then again, we are explorers after all. Not only can students at the school buy books, clothing, gadgets, supplies and huskies, etc. they can also get them gift-wrapped. (Not the huskies. They don't like it much.)

Solar panels fit round the back here.

### THE "VON STRUDELHOPF" ARCTIC SURVIVAL JACKET

Light, and waterproof, this jacket has been specifically designed by the staff of the School of Exploration and Survival to be perfect for all environments. (Well, not all. It wouldn't be much good underwater. It's not that waterproof.) It has thirty-two pockets, five of which are so well hidden we haven't found them yet. The jacket comes with built in satellite phone transmitter, wi-fi, solar panels on the back. And a small espresso coffee machine. Also you can use the hood as a water filter.

## EQUIPMENT

### THE SNOWMASTER HUSKY/SLED COMBO

For the arctic explorer. A three meter dog sled with all huskies ready-attached. (Warning: the huskies are not house-trained. Do not try to sneak them into your dormitory.)

### THE DESERTMASTER CAMEL/SLED COMBO

This is, frankly, the same as the Snowmaster. Only without the huskies. And with a camel. (Be warned: the camel is even less house-trained than the huskies.)

### THE MOUNTAIN MASTER DONKEY/WAGON COMBO.

It's like the Snowmaster but with a... oh, work it out yourself.

### KIPPERBUNG'S COMPASS 33

This new model from Kipperbung was thought to be useless, as in manufacturing it, they accidentally reversed the magnetic field. Actually it is now extremely useful to anyone heading south.

Take Compass 33 if you are heading to Antartica.

## ■ BOOKS

We stock a wide selection of books. Some of our bestsellers include

### THE KIPPERBUNG COMPLETE ALPHABETICAL GUIDE TO THE COUNTRIES OF THE WORLD

Doesn't really live up to the title as the section beginning with the letter C got missed out. So if you're thinking of going to Canada, Cameroon, the Central African Republic, China, etc. you might want to get a different book.

### MY LIFE ON ICE, VON STRUDELHOPF

An account of the Professor's life, including his many expeditions and his attempt to get a world Globe soccer tournament going.

### COOKING FOR EXPLORERS, MRS. VON STRUDELHOPF

Sixty recipes guaranteed to encourage your explorer to go wandering.

### THE LOST LIBRARIAN

The amazing but true story of how a librarian was attacked by a polar bear and fell down a ravine and how she survived by eating the novels of Agatha Christie which she happened to have with her.

## ■ FOOD

### SURVIVO FOODS FROM NOODLES R US

A line of specially prepared survival foods, packed in vacuum sealed bags. Just heat and eat.

Flavours include
•Chicken and Noodle
•Ham and Noodle
•Cabbage and Noodle
•Noodle, Ham, Chicken, Cabbage and more Noodle
•Poodle and noodle (Not really, we just liked the rhyme.)
•Shepherd's Pie (Lamb and Potato)
•Chinese Shepherds Pie (Lamb, Potato and Noodle)
And many more. Mostly involving noodle.

**EXTRAS**

# CLUBS AND SOCIETIES

**The School of Exploration and Survival has many clubs and societies that may be of interest to you. Check the boxes for those you'd like to join.**

### ☐ GOING VERY FAST DOWNHILL SOCIETY

For anyone interested in skiing, snowboarding, bobsledding, etc.

Where: Ski Lodge, Amazing Academy mountain range
When: Wednesday 2:30 p.m. or whenever the snow has fallen and you can ditch class

### ☐ EXTREME JOGGING

Make keeping fit more interesting. Join us for a jog across the desert, down tunnels, through caves, and, once a year, through crocodile-infested rivers. (Although that's more "sprinting" than "jogging.")

Where: Amazing Academy Jungle
When: Fridays 6 p.m.

### ☐ LOST CITIES SOCIETY

For anyone interested in tracing lost cities and civilizations. Recent expeditions have searched for Atlantis, Shangri-La, and Coventry.

Where: The Library
When: Wednesdays 8 p.m.

### ☐ THE MR. SNOOKUMS SOCIETY

Is your soft animal interested in survival skills? Come and introduce your teddy bear/ragdoll/cuddly pterodactyl to Mr. Snookums and discuss how best to use soft animals in survival situations.

Where: Survival Dept
When: Tuesday lunchtimes

VON STRUDELHOPF SAYS, "AND SO WE REACH THE END OF THE BASIC COURSE FOR EXPLORATION AND SURVIVAL. MAY I THANK ALL STUDENTS FOR THEIR HARD WORK – YOU HAVE ALL BEEN A CREDIT TO THE SCHOOL. NOW THE TASK IS TO TAKE WHAT YOU HAVE LEARNED AND USE IT WISELY. GO FROM HERE AND START EXPLORING. ASK QUESTIONS, SEEK OUT BEAUTY, AIM FOR UNDERSTANDING; AND TREAT PEOPLE AND PLACES WITH RESPECT. AND, WHEREVER POSSIBLE, LEAVE THE WORLD A BETTER PLACE THAN YOU FOUND IT."